T0345218

IN SPITE OF THE DARK SILENCE

In Spite of
the Dark Silence

Jorge Volpi

Translated and with an Afterword by Olivia Maciel

SWAN ISLE PRESS
CHICAGO

Jorge Volpi Escalante is one of the founders of the "Crack Movement" (Generación del crack) in Mexico and author of several well-known novels, including *In Search of Klingsor* and *Season of Ash*. Volpi has been awarded the Spanish literary prize, Premio Biblioteca Breve, and the French Deux-Océans-Grinzane-Cavour prize. *A pesar del oscuro silencio* (*In Spite of the Dark Silence*) is his first novel.

Olivia Maciel is professor of Spanish and Latin American literature at Loyola University-Chicago and is also on the faculty of the Honors College at the University of Illinois–Chicago. Her works include *Surrealismo en la poesia de Xavier Villaurrutia, Octavio Paz, y Luis Cernuda. Mexico (1926-1963)* and *Shadow in Silver / Sombra en plata* (Swan Isle Press).

Swan Isle Press, Chicago 60640-8790

©2010 by Swan Isle Press

All rights reserved. Published 2010

Printed in the United States of America
First Edition

14 13 12 11 10   12345
ISBN-13: 978-0-9748881-8-7 (cloth)

Originally published as *A pesar del oscuro silencio*, ©Editorial Joaquín Mortiz, 1992

Grateful acknowledgment is made to Claudio Isaac Rueda for his illustration, "Retrato de Jorge Cuesta" which appears on the jacket and interior of this edition.

Library of Congress Cataloging-in-Publication Data

Volpi Escalante, Jorge,
 [A pesar del oscuro silencio. English]
 In spite of the dark silence / Jorge Volpi ; translated and with an afterword by Olivia Maciel. -- 1st ed.
  p. cm.
 Includes bibliographical references.
 ISBN 978-0-9748881-8-7 (alk. paper)
 1. Cuesta, Jorge, 1903-1942--Fiction. I. Maciel, Olivia, II. Title.
 PQ7298.32.O47P413 2010
 863'.64--dc22
                         2010042780

Swan Isle Press gratefully acknowledges that this book has been made possible, in part, with the support of generous grants from:

• The Illinois Arts Council, A State of Illinois Agency
• Europe Bay Giving Trust

www.swanislepress.com

To my parents
To Eloy Urroz and Luis García Vallarta

CONTENTS

In Spite of
the Dark Silence

FIRST OEUVRE
The Sign of a Hand

I awaken in me what I've been
to become silence and nothing.

CUESTA

1

His name was Jorge, like mine, and for that his life hurts me twice. I didn't know him yet, had never seen his picture or barely glanced at any of his poems, but upon learning how he'd died—a trivial anecdote in the debris of a distant conversation—I had a precise image of his face, his hands, his torments. While I listened to the remnants of the talk and my pupils perambulated the smoke of cigarettes, I saw him clearly—better yet: I saw through him, in his room, two men in white waiting impatiently for him. Two beings made of wax, of gestures as opaque as their wills, sitting on a frayed sofa; in front of them against the light, the thin body of the poet, sober and light as a prayer. I'd observe his fingers dancing slowly and hear his voice—no, the echo of his voice—asking them, may the paradox be worth it, for a bit more time; he needs to get ready and finish a task that still worries him.

The nurses tell him it's all right, he has ten minutes, and not to try anything (as if he had any strength to escape); then they remain immobile, looking at paintings and shelves, old books and dust, trapped in the eyes of that ghost fallen to pieces. Ten minutes; enough time to prepare ten different ways of dying, or fail at nine attempts and make best use of the last one. Hesitant, the poet enters the bathroom and fastens the door lock; they notice the pin's sliding sound with indifference, prisoners of the timeless time of that unique afternoon, the emptiness which separates instants.

Inside, the poet looks at his double self in the mirror: under his eyelashes, under the injured eyelid on his left cheek, the signs of exhaustion; he is dirty and wears a beard growth of many days. Nonetheless, his expression isn't one of fear but of acceptance. Inscribed in lightning, his whole life travels in front of his pain.

He feels he is about to cry. On a corner of the sink rests the blade; on the other the foamy soap and a ruffled shaving brush. The steel blade attracts him with its gleam of rain. He takes it and without hesitation, with one dry motion, carries it to his bare neck. Why not once and for all? Why not end definitely with the anguish and the memory, his image? It would be sufficient to increase the pressure to forget the panic and the cold with a slash. In a few seconds everything would be consummated forever. He doesn't lack valor, he is excessively sad. The henchmen awaiting him—those that allowed him, disobeying the rules, to go into the bathroom—are blameless; they are not the ones who must pay for his blood, least of all when it's not ready to be spilled. Something more valuable than suicide detains him and calms him. He is logical: instead of killing himself, he shaves with a craftsman's precision. Afterward, he wipes off his face, rinses, dresses, and buttons his shirt. He then leaves the bathroom as if no thought had crossed his mind.

He pleads again to the watchmen for a bit more time: he must conclude his creation before accepting the abysms of despair. The nurses, fascinated by his tone, the firmness of his request and the sensation of witnessing an ineffable sacrifice, submissively accept. They risk their job, their negligence breaking all rules, but they are incapable of resisting, horror has absolutely won them over. Imminently frozen, they sit with blank brains. The clock marks the exact time, its tick tock vanishing.

Anxious, the poet walks toward the rickety chest on the side of the bed, takes a notebook out of a drawer and tears out three pages. The light begins to dim: in the room only a few orange and purple glints trap the silhouette of a pen on the covers. Leaning on top of the chest, the poet focuses on the whiteness of the three pages; there he finds the vestiges of his fantasies, their whispers, mysteries, opaque tranquilities. On the notebook he pours the minuscule drops of ink that slowly become the last verses of a poem, the "Song to a Mineral God," the obsession of his life.

That is the fruit whose master is time. He writes to conclude his creation and his existence; three strophes, eighteen starkly jotted lines before entering the lunatic asylum. Each word carefully distilled, burns more than a wound; in it—a limit closer to the precipice—he has deposited his lucidity and weeping, his only arms; his confession and last will and testament. After the last period, with the same calmness, with equal pride, he allows himself to be taken by those men; he knows it isn't they who sequester him, he is beyond any prison. That is how his destiny ends. Just a few days later he emasculates himself and finally commits suicide during an unending dawn of August.

The story, spread during a trivial conversation, enwrapped me immediately, and then unhinged me with the violence of its images and the acidity of its sense. Who was that poet? Who was, indeed, Jorge Cuesta? Fugitive of the cigarette smoke and of alcohol's vapor, caught in an impossible discussion, all I had left was the restlessness of one who parts without knowing where to.

But his name was Jorge, like me, and that's why his life started to doubly hurt me.

2

I stopped writing late, as usual; I didn't even shave, I took the car keys and I left the house. I arrived at the concert hall, already in dim lights. The reflectors made the musicians on stage appear tense and nervous.

To get to my place I had to distract various bodies, who getting up or shrinking would resist my weight between the seats. I knew that my fuss bothered her, taking her away from the musical notation and from the cello, making her eyes turn toward the darkness, but I didn't care. Just a few minutes later her left hand swayed the bow as if the world surged from that gesture.

Tired, convinced that all there was for me to do was to await the end of the concert, I tried to concentrate on the sepia glint of the instruments and the tension of the strings to evade the back and forth of the sound, though the tedium grew beyond my best efforts. At the end of a horrible day I was not in the mood to withstand a session expressly designed for boredom, a program where Schoenberg was the most comforting and the night turned into a nightmare. Not even Alma's face, faintly outlined between her black dress and the dark background, was sufficient to keep me awake.

I sat back, incapable of putting up with the boredom, far away from her. Nevertheless, as soon as I stood away from the shadow of the spectators and performers my anguish receded. Almost by accident I stumbled upon the music that floated toward me imperceptibly. Suddenly Schoenberg was able to envelop me: I followed him in the air, completing his jumps and bridges, submerging myself in the lines he traced in space. Then, when I was starting to enjoy it, when I had made it my own, I understood that music didn't exist in reality. Modeled in time, time destroys it: each phrase, each compass, each note is dissolved in its immediateness. It hurts to think that only the dark mind of man saves music from its emptiness. Music is not pleasure, but the unstable memory of pleasure; little would we care to listen to it for an instant, if we were not conscious of the previous seconds. It was just a memory game, a sharp remembrance, such as the stars we continue admiring in spite of their having exploded millions of years ago. The clapping of an indifferent public raised me from the stupor of my ruminations. Alma and her colleagues left the stage for a second and returned to fainter clapping.

The lights were turned on and suddenly the concert hall emptied.

Alma came out of the dressing room soon thereafter; she'd taken off her make-up and loosened her hair, she carried on her shoulder a case with her musical instrument. I kissed her guardedly, and took her cello as we walked in silence toward the exit.

We got into the car. She went over the concert and tried not to scold me for my interruption or poor interest. It was always the same thing. We wouldn't search for answers for the incessant questions the other would have. Alma wished to measure the very low spirits that paralyzed her, while I for my part didn't consider it my business. Considering ourselves unique, each in their own right, we would avoid offering solace to each other. Our love—if any of it still remained—transformed itself, from a conversation without words into delirious soliloquies.

We got out of the car, climbed the stairs, and went into the apartment. Neither of us turned on the light. We wanted to go to sleep, but more selfishly than it appeared, we decided to hold each other. We abandoned ourselves to the moment as if we wished to escape from each other rather than find each other and were awarded the last ten seconds before total destruction: desire annulled us to such an extent that it exploded one more time. Just like the stars we gaze at, though they no longer exist, we saw our love explode despite its having been emptied years ago.

3

I see him stretched out on the bed, pale and frail, his hands hidden under the sheet, tenderly placed on his belly. He seems a statue about to emerge from the marble of the bed, in any case, one more entity in the furnishings of the room and not a living thing. It's not even noticeable when his lungs swell out or when his eyelids tremble at times. Nevertheless, an uncertain glint escapes his gaze, as if in that mutilated, worn out and broken body there still remained a remnant of peace, of the secret fire that always nourished him.

Surrounding him there is a dense and infinite whiteness of a blinding pulchritude: the floor, roof, walls are inseparable from the intense luminosity. Even the slightest shadow has been eliminated, not a single corner remains under shadows. The doctors have forbidden him the only rest to which a human being has a right: sleep.

The poet resists and tries to forget, but the reflectors, carefully pointing at him, prevent him from doing so; not without the intention of punishment, he has been condemned to a permanent vigil. This is a good image of that eternity he has yearned for so very long; there is no sense of movement, tension, or flux, space itself dissolves into a mirror without borders. Only in a place such as this one, outside of the world, can remain an incomplete creature, a monster made asexual by his own will. The neutral space is made for a neutral body.

Only a few hours ago he rested with apparent serenity in some friends house out by the *Desierto de los leones*, where he was taken, to recover his health as in an amiable prison. There, he could be looked after and attended with great care; with the fear and respect one has for that which is incomprehensible. Everyone thought that he would get better with the cold wind and the forest, but the result was opposite: the pressure in his head became unbearable, memories tortured him. The discharges of violence weren't so sudden, since they emanated from the wells of his loneliness; already, on some other occasion he had to get away from his son, to not love him and destroy him in the explosion of his overflowing lust.

Stretched out on the bed, pale and frail, his hands hidden under the sheets, gently placed on his belly, he finds himself in one of the most distant rooms of Doctor Lavista's hospital in Tlalpan, surrounded by orchards in ruins and crumbling haciendas. He was brought in by nervous male nurses that in their panic don't know whether to wish him a prompt recovery or a quick death at the sight of his mutilated organs.

But what does he think of the fatality that has overcome him? What does he feel; shame, pain, fear? Perhaps a stark regret, vainly directed, whose origin he barely recognizes. In his face—he resembles the livid face of angels—it's impossible to read any word, any accusation, and any human trace. He has become another cause of silence: impossible to make any sense of his acts. It's better to keep quiet.

He rises with great effort; he stands, and then kneels on the floor, next to the window. On his knees on the floor, he gathers his hands in front of his thorax, lowers his chin, pursuing a childish fervor. Before his closed eyelids he observes the saints of the churches in Córdoba, the awe of the chalice, the tears of repentance. Imperceptibly, the chiaroscuro of the cupolas and the fire of the holy wafer seep into the cell with the frozen and incomplete perfume of ruins. But he doesn't get even one tear out of the weeping that moved him not long ago. Instead of a prayer, a prolonged tremor caresses his closed lips, a gentle breeze that doesn't turn into sound. Instead, though his devotions crash into the ceiling, in his interior, there prays an authentic zeal.

Lord, our destiny is written from the beginning, he writes on a piece of paper to his sister. He remembers her gaze and loves her with desperation. He wants to hold onto those eyes, to be saved with them. How could we deny ourselves to it? We are bound to it, and with no more protection than your mercy. He wants to shout but his mouth tastes of ashes. His skin exudes each syllable, each letter: Oh God, our Lord who wants to offer us shelters, without leaving homeless any of us who are your servants.

How much time did he spend kneeling, finding out that his penitence was useless and deaf? How many years suffering that agony? His slow breathing shuts off time; the distance between inhalations and exhalations dilate the minutes. Thought is not bound to becoming.

Finally he makes up his mind. From the nearby rooms it is possible to hear shouting capable of crumbling thick walls; incomprehensible, bestial voices, the only portion of those creatures that escapes to freedom. The noises are burdensome; he wishes for silence to keep him company once and for all. But not even the distant pain is able to shake him: sensations have dissolved. He doesn't feel, nor remember, nor suffer, nor weep. Almost by instinct, by inertia, he ties a few sheets and hangs himself from the headrest of the bed. The taste darkness distills is the proper sense that inhabits others and dominates the future.

4

I couldn't sleep, perturbation had been too intense. I'd been shown the luminescence of the body, and at the same time its immediate death. It was the most intense combat of our life because we both sensed it was a last opportunity. Beyond a second, a thousandth of a second, pleasure turned into pain. My wish had been to retain the sensation, to freeze the orgasm, with or through Alma: I did—that's what I think—at least for an instant. Slowly the memory vanished into uncertainty: Did it really exist? Did I win? How to prove it? It was impossible to be sure, memory was the only witness. Time took away my certainty: the joy the instant turns into is only survived by the thirst that wishes for it; nothing of it remains, but its absence, the bizarre will to recover what is lost.

Alma slept till seven. Her reddened eyes hardly retained a certain beauty. Their gray pearl oscillated between a blue and a green, depending on her mood: they would darken with tiredness and laughter, brighten with crying or lust.

During two years Alma lived with an orchestra conductor who left her without saying why. Every day, feverishly, she would analyze the nuances of the relationship, not so much to figure out whom to blame than to find an answer. She never did. In another case she would have given up, but facing uncertainty it was useless temptation to do so. She left her position in the orchestra and even thought of abandoning music altogether; she was stopped by the anguish of the unknown. But ever since, she began to play in a manner that expressed her devastation, as if she could take it out on the absence of words.

It was at that time that we met, and I accepted she would not love me as she loved him; it wasn't within her power to escape his influence. My jealousy, almost conquered, would catch a sense of impotence: hatred for what I couldn't control, the useless, and the gratuitous. Out of kilter, trapped by a number of limited possibilities, we didn't cease to love the wrong person (I with Alma, she with the conductor and perhaps he with another woman who could love me). But we preferred to overlook this defeat knowing that it was impossible to steal ourselves from this delirium. There was little we could do to overcome this, our most minimal efforts turning into daily ashes. Without talking to each other, without a fight, we lived an existence marked by musical notation and literature—my harmless profession—more than by our own will. We would come together in the evening among vain caresses and a pleasure which seemed more like an obligation. If not love—in all manners certain—at least we had its opaque image in our bodies.

Enjoyment became absurd; it wasn't a matter of reciprocity, or duty—toward her but more particularly toward my own pride. Instead of delaying the search for pleasure, pleasure lay in its constant search, in movement. Not to become an owner of the explosion, but to intuit its happening, because in the end, thirst is all that remains, and disappointment. In the end the slow and fixated intuition of pleasure doesn't cease to be pleasure, to be nothing.

5

Slowly I allowed myself to become entrapped by Cuesta's oeuvre; I got his poems, a biography and began asking my friends about him. They told me little. One Sunday, fed up with our disenchantment, I invited Alma to visit his tomb. I wanted to do away once and for all with that painful type of truce that mediated between us, and the idea seemed strange enough to make it happen. Briefly I told her what I knew about him till now, his death at the hands of literature.

—Yes, to the cemetery—I said; her expression didn't make me back down.

After dinner—the food tasted less bitter than I'd thought— we made our way to the French Cemetery, *Viaducto* and *Cuauhtémoc*, next to the baseball field. Nearly five in the afternoon, the last rays of sunlight slid among the mildewed walls of the site. In front of the desolate avenue the main gate read, *Heureux qui meurt dans le Seigneur*, its guardians the flower vendors, traffickers of that fleeting contact between the dead and those still alive.

In spite of my initial desire for peace, Alma's growing irritation pleased me, as if it were a scolding to her vanity. The sky began to cloud and a wind gust hit us in the face.—This is all we needed—she said. I walked ahead toward the administrative office, a greenish hole of a hut in which a man dozed off oblivious to the sleep of his charges. When Alma caught up with me, the clerk had already agreed to show me his register, though he warned me he'd never heard of a Jorge Cuesta and had never noticed his grave. Under the scrutiny of Alma's chastising gaze, we went over the yellowish pages in vain. Cuesta was refusing to share space with those names. Irritated, the man agreed to take us to the eastern part of the cemetery, behind the church, where it was probable that the body of a suicide could be found. The wind was getting closer to turning into a storm and the improvised guide announced that it was almost closing time. Nevertheless we crossed a long avenue of broken semi-buried headstones, and truncated skeletons; Christs and Virgins followed us, their disenchantment trapped in the white stone they'd been torn from. We were the only intruders in that island safe from the hours; not even the birds dared to interfere with the dense and rainy calm.

Grumbling, the custodian left us in an area of low monuments and frayed crosses, a few meters from the wall at the back of the cemetery. We began the search, but suddenly Alma stopped short, restless.

—I'm fed up. I'll wait for you outside—she said, and left.

It had already gotten dark as I stood in front of the small sepulcher that kept, under a broken ash tree, the remains of the poet. 1904–1942, stated the stone, and then—though now I don't know if these words appeared there, or if later I placed them there mistakenly—the following inscrutable epitaph, written by Xavier Villaurrutia in the serene knowledge of insanity:

> I sharpened reason
> so much, that obscure
> it became for everyone else
> my life, my passion,
> and my madness.

They say that I've died.
I won't ever die:
I'm awake!

As soon as I'd recovered from the momentary cold and madness, I thought I heard approaching footsteps, crushing the dry leaves of eucalyptus. It couldn't be Alma. I retreated behind a tree trunk.

As if the path was known from memory, a shadow—only the night makes me assume it was dressed in a black overcoat—made its way among the crypts. It seemed to make a stop by the side of the tomb. I left with the feeling of having attended a grotesque rendezvous, though there may have been nobody there.

6

Monday, facing again the rickety desk, buried under useless memos and a suffocating tedium. Clocks agonized; their immobile hands set out to trap us in work that although light, wouldn't escape routine, humidity and rust. The office would slip away through the hollow walls of an old building of very high ceilings and low-level saltpeter. Tubular chairs and tables disseminated their worn-out shine against the dying light.

I sat down and waited a bit before I began to rock my chair on its hind legs. Life is to be there, as fixatedly as the frozen and transparent height pretends it to be when it climbs. Fed up, I'd make an effort to put Cuesta's life in order in bits of paper that were cuttings from official minutes and memorandums; I'd write significant dates, the works and comments of some of his critics, but in the end I knew they didn't amount to much. They barely were useful glimmers to pass the hours. But those sketches wouldn't piece together a single idea: years and names turned insignificant inside that polluted air of bureaucrats and secretaries.

True, I was not responsible, the salary was low but not too much, and in essence I could do whatever I felt like; nonetheless, that abandonment was enough to destroy my spirit. Cornered, I couldn't understand why I'd remained in that job, what insane wish for security obligated me to continue amidst all that shit.

Alma. In the end all I was doing was to entangle myself in old frictions with her, failed arguments, reproaches. There is no solidity that can withstand such pressure, even the slightest shadow magnifies the disagreements, the incompatibility that resolved in obsessive complaints. For hours I went over the same wound of the week. The chamber music festival of San Miguel? Fine, but don't ask me to come with you. Do you think I don't have anything else to do? That imbecile is not important to me, as you know, and he should not be important to you either. He is the conductor, period. Forget it; I don't want to go on with this.

And then onward, to foresee the cumulus of variants, oppositions, incomplete circles. Why not simply explode without being nasty and give some leeway to our apathy? — something that would cause us to give in, to break the vain sense of our fights. But we had to be impartial, fair, made of ice. To overcome obstacles as if they didn't exist, to let them pass; the worm-eaten jealousy, the switched-off rage, hatred more intense. To concede, always, in peace, in silence, with full and precise indifference.

That's why I detested those slow battles that kept me dauntless, in such vexation. Instead of keeping up with my readings, with my obscure job as a writer, I would pursue uncertain wanderings. I shuffled again the pile of papers with the information, and selected one at random: Guadalupe Marín: Cuesta's wife from 1928 to 1932, before she married Diego Rivera; author of *La única* (The Only One), a veiled autobiography in which she takes vengeance against the poet; frivolous, without a sense of borders, tenacious; see her portrait by Diego.

Just to lengthen the charade I dove into the phone book for her name. I imagined myself visiting her, knocking at her door timidly, threshing out her memories, taking hold of her ghosts. Lupe Marín. Green eyes. I could plot anything, provided it took me away from myself.

7

The white stone barely showed among the walls of the other buildings, like a mediocre intruder sliding into a sad zone of dry mansions and deserted avenues. It was coated with a dignity of perfect harmonies that soon dispersed the initial disappointment. A large door of red cedar attracted the eye to the center of the façade, encrusted with medieval door knockers and minuscule ogives; all the way around, the insurmountable stone extended itself, for even the windows had been shuttered, making the glass and wrought iron disappear. I didn't hesitate to place my hand in one of those iron rings, shattering it against the beams that sustained it, but as soon as I did, the knocks sank into my head, widening with the confused information I had on Guadalupe Marín. I made an effort to remember the brushstrokes of Rivera and the scarce impressions that Cuesta had left of this woman of long fingers, feverish gaze, and smoky voice, but really, I wasn't able to guess the volume of her features. What would remain of the temperamental diva, activist, and model? What would have been preserved, after fifty years, of her courage, of the insults directed against Cuesta, of her weeping and the dense pain upon abandoning him, of the rancor, of the lines she wrote to avenge herself? How much pride, how many deaf tears, how much accumulated remorse in her flesh since then?

It dawned on me I was about to face her and wasn't ready, with impunity she would bring forth the petrified memory of the poet. I'd allowed myself to be carried away by a sudden impulse. I didn't know what to tell her or ask her, how to present myself to her. Speak to me about Cuesta. That would have been enough for her to throw me out without thinking about it twice. Forgive me, but I'm obsessed with... even worse. My perspiration drowned me when a voice asked my name from behind the wooden door.

—What?—I mumbled.

—Who is it?—the voice asked again.

—Jorge—I exclaimed without paying attention to the awkward answer and didn't say anything else. Soon I realized the immense mistake.

—Come in—I heard incredulously, and a maid opened the door.

I crossed the threshold and came into an extensive patio bound by a garden. The house, positioned in a corner, seemed a cube adorned with capitals, pre-Hispanic forms, worn out sculptures and stone beehives.

A new entrance led me into the interior as if instead of advancing I were retreating in time: century-old furniture, finely polished, inhabited the reduced space of the living room; wicker chairs, tables, velvet sofas, display cabinets, and shelves, found shelter among those walls. Very heavy curtains, the color of sherry, kept the room in a dark penumbra, only tarnished by innumerable mirrors exchanging glimmers.

Confused by the tireless repetition of her image in portraits and mirrors, I thought I saw a woman seated in a high armchair at the back of the room. A difficult breathing gave away the artificer of that landscape built with the spoils of her mind. I could barely see her blouse, her gray hair and her age.

She held her hands on her lap, the hands of a pianist and vendor of flowers, of a poet and magician.

—What do you want from me?—I suddenly heard. I was unable to respond.

—What do you want from me?

Perhaps without realizing it, the elderly woman had suspended time, the only obsession of the man she'd been married to. She let out a flawed grimace and returned to the stubbornness with which she greeted me.

—If you only knew how I've waited for this—she said, and I understood that she wasn't talking to the present— but now it's too late. I remain here, getting old while you have gone—she mumbled to herself in rapture—. I don't feel disdain for you, I'm only afraid; afraid of seeing this face of mine, these hands; afraid of remaining all alone with your death. I didn't dare interrupt her delirium, her prolonged agony in each word.

—Jorge—she continued, —I don't want to spurn you, as I don't want to love you. I'm here because of you, because of your stubborn insistence on being like me. Jorge, Jorge, Jorge…

And for an instant, sunk into the distance and in pain, I noticed the wrinkled wince of Cuesta weeping in all the paintings.

—Jorge—she said, yet with thick lips that were not her own— I've lost all hope.

8

I sense he is nearby crouching, hiding in each shadow, in the same places I visit, in my conversations, in my books. There he is, cold, constant, and impassive. I'm invaded by his atrocious intelligence, his madness, my panic. He is a demon that doesn't laugh, but yearns, and remembers. A nostalgic sinner that hovers over me: his mission is to lead me astray, to infect me with his sad repentance. He is in the cemetery and prays next to the poet's tomb, I also find him at work, in street corners, in concert halls, and in mirrors. I'm not kidding myself: he exists. He is the beholder of truth, of the supreme secret, of knowledge.

I wake up.

I transcribe the biography of Panabiére (*Itinerary of Dissidence. Jorge Cuesta 1903-1942*):

Life of Jorge Cuesta

Established on the basis of testimonies, correspondence and archives:

1903. He is born in Córdoba, Veracruz, on September 21st.
1904. Fall and lesion of the left eye.
1909. Enrollment in the private school *Unión*.
1912. He concludes elementary school in the public school *América*.
1925-1921. He undertakes middle and upper level studies in Córdoba's High School.

1921. He arrives in Mexico City and enrolls in the Faculty of Chemistry at the *Universidad Nacional Autónoma de México.*

1923. In April, he is appointed delegate to the Student Council. In May he becomes the Director of the journal *Ciencias Químicas.*

1924. In July, he publishes in *Antena* the short story "Don Francisco's Resurrection."

1925. Last exam at the Faculty. He doesn't turn in the thesis that would have qualified him to receive the title of chemical engineer.

1926. He takes a position as chemist in the hacienda *El Potrero*, in Córdoba. He returns to the capital in November.

1927. In April, thanks to Bernardo Gastélum, he becomes an employee of the Council of Public Health. He lasts a month. At year's end he meets Guadalupe Marín.

1928. He writes articles for the literary magazine *Ulises* and the preface for the *Antología* of Contemporáneos. In May, he leaves for Paris, with stops in Havana and London. In June, he arrives in Paris; he takes lodging at the Suez Hotel, on Boulevard Saint Michel. He meets André Breton and Robert Desnos; visits frequently with other Mexican artists who are also in Paris: Carlos Pellicer, Samuel Ramos, Agustín Lazo. In August he returns to Mexico, where he marries Lupe Marín.

1929. Beginning in July he lives in Córdoba with Lupe and works at the hacienda *El Potrero*.

1930. He is named chief of laboratories at the National Society of Sugar and Alcohol.

1940. First fit of madness. Persecution complex.

1942. Second fit of madness: self-castration and subsequent internment at Doctor Lavista's sanatorium in Tlalpan. On August 13th, at 3:25 a.m. he commits suicide.

9

Just a few kilometers away from our destination and I still didn't understand how I'd allowed myself to be convinced. San Miguel de Allende irritated me for its false showing of intellectuals and artists, and most of all for its festival of chamber music, atrociously solemn, that made me visit it. But more than feeling hatred toward Alma, I despised myself for having accepted or more so for not having had the will to resist her disdain.

The steering wheel burned my hands before a road that extended itself, diaphanous, as if it were the infinite cloistered between two mirrors. It was as if it would never reach the yellowing grasses and clouds that led toward its shadows. I had an asphyxiating premonition of not being able to free myself from the arrogance of Barrientos, his slouched posture and his alcoholic breath even when he conducts. But this time I'd decided to ignore him as if there weren't registers of Alma in his memory. Along the way, we didn't snatch even one word from each other; just as I did, Alma preserved with extreme caution the delicate equilibrium that kept us linked to each other.

Any pretext would have been enough to hurl us against the days and the apologies. Despite the delirious perspiration that swayed her hair—and the desire trapped in my hands—our relationship wouldn't be able to withstand a sharp word or remark.

—We've arrived—she said uncomfortably, not far from the first towers of San Miguel.

We stopped at the lodge and registered immediately. Alma went to take a shower and I headed to the bar. Dozens of persons I attempted to not recognize drank aperitifs at small crowded colonial tables. I asked for a beer and sat in a corner toward the back of the room, near a terrace. I yearned for a bit of calmness, but instead Barrientos showed up with his amiable sense of superiority and his unshaven face. Behind his humidified eyes and a mechanical smile he approached me.

—Jorge, what a pleasure—He didn't wait for a response and sat next to me—. When did you arrive? Alma told me that you had to work and she didn't know if…

—She went upstairs, she'll be back soon.

He called the waiter by name and ordered a whiskey. He wore, as always, the same mustard corduroy jacket with which I remembered him; his voice was the same that I used to curse on the phone. They brought his drink and in one gulp he swallowed more than half of it. He paused, asked about my job, and wetted his lips again. His talk didn't accomplish anything else other than to lengthen the minutes, attenuate the wait with his levity.

Soon Alma arrived, with a blouse of gauze and wet hair. Barrientos waved at her—you look wonderful—his voice resounded welcoming her, partially standing up.

I couldn't tell if he was taking me for an imbecile, or simply didn't give a damn. Irritated, Alma positioned herself between the two of us. She tried to ease things, exchanging a pair of complicit glances. She ordered a *sangría* and the three of us began to exchange evasive comments, how is the office, well, and the orchestra, also well, thank you, so much work, contracts with the soloists, terrible, yes, perfect health…Finally, Barrientos suggested we have dinner somewhere else.

—You both go—I beat them to it—. I prefer to rest a while. I'll see you at the concert.

Alma listened with hidden hate; I left without understanding exactly what I had done, but with a certain sense of satisfaction. Had it not been so bitter, Alma's countenance would have been comical: in the end I had only carried out her will to its last consequences.

Under a sun that destroyed me, I went out for a walk thinking about Cuesta, obstinately thinking about Cuesta.

10

I walked aimlessly, sometimes chasing my shadow, sometimes being chased by it, guided more by the stones than by my
own wishes. The ochres and maroons from the earth vanished
in the walls of the hovels, facing, as a cluster, an almost marine
sky. The painful calm of the sun stopped time, the instant cal-
cinations in the ardent gravel. Without a trace of movement—
except for my steps— the landscape undulated. What could one
think in such moments? Not in them, of course, but not too
much on the poet either. It was enough to imagine him in the
deserted side streets of Córdoba bearing the clouds in his eyes
to forget the rest. To transform what is vile in what is noble; to
flee from what is transitory. How could he know, then, while
he meandered, that these ideas would lead him to his own end?
Perhaps his weakened intelligence was not able to acknowledge
the end result of his behavior, lucidity blinded him.

His life also seemed, in that manner, a path, a road tragi-
cally accepted, a challenge of fire. The sense of his search re-
sided in walking, in being displaced, in advancing. The road as
its own explanation, without a beginning or an end, without
shores. The will to abolish history as an attempt, nothing more.

Without realizing it, as if my legs led the way, I walked a
long distance, and found myself in an unknown area. My eyelids hurt and not a glimmer of San Miguel appeared in sight.
The lightness of my digressions dragged me along. Exhausted,
I slipped into an abandoned shed amidst the foliage. A kind of
lost silo. I entered the stone building, but a few minutes passed

before the sun left my pupils allowing me to look at the dust on the walls. From its large windows came a milky and wan air; on the floor, straw embroidered carpets and some puddles invented seas in the corners.

Darkness gave me back my breathing; inside, the world's death rattle didn't gain access, not even the afternoon's heat found room there. I had completely forgotten the concert that was about to start in San Miguel: the damp beams were good enough to forget any sound, any disturbance. Their beauty diverted me to the cobwebs, the remains of a small oven and furniture buried under the sand. The world opened itself to my body: its grandeur hidden inside those moldy walls. Everything—except me—seemed ensconced according to a superior order, perfect, whose stability broke my previous conviction that I should run away. The straw, the wood and the stone found their counterpart in the smoke, the interior paleness and the announced death of the sunset. This was the truth that had fascinated Cuesta. I touched the wet clay, amazed by the eloquence of the revelation:

My sight diffused on the space is space itself.

And I fell asleep this time thinking of Alma, stubbornly thinking of Alma.

11

So much time exchanging misgivings and turbid smiles, of working together without looking at each other, of avoiding encounters and excessive words so that now they can sit facing each other, in the same place as before, waiting for something that will save them from explanations. This is the first time in five years they see each other alone, as nervous as when they used to meet at the orchestra in the mornings, hiding the memory of having awakened together.

Disguising wounds, they mistakenly recover the futilities of the past, the vengeances, and the reconciliations. Perhaps also, some instants of rage and music mixed with the sharp images of separation. Everything ended like a symphony concluding after a two hour outburst: with the absolute desolation of silence. But they attempt not to remember, not to repeat the previous scenes; they avoid disputes they never had.

—This program always causes fear in me—he says—. I don't know why.

In love (because in spite of forgetfulness, this can't be anything but that) the will of the parties disappears little by little as much as they make an effort. It's not they who master what they do, say, or don't do. They are carried, unknowingly, by a circumstance that in its human stupidity almost redeems them.

She asks:

—What was the reason?

He doesn't answer. And though in reality neither of them wishes to speak, they are incapable of resisting the temptation, accusations are posed. The transparency of a minute obligates them to betray a justified muteness of many years.

He realizes how useless words will be, that their actions—as anyone's—don't deserve justifications. Nevertheless she falls.

—One motive—she insists.

There's no alternative but to lie. He insinuates he doesn't understand it either, that he has forgotten the cause, or that perhaps there never was one, that she was not to blame, it was an impetuous and visceral decision; to please forgive him. But in his last show of pride he assumes responsibility.

—We're not getting anywhere—he ends, smelling of alcohol, transformed into alcohol.

She repeats it, concealing her plot.

Then they eat and drink coffee as if they had never offended each other and as if time and pain were a game. In the end, instead, they know that the opposite is true.

An hour later he conducts her in a rehearsal, and afterward in the gala concert of the festival, but truly, it is she who from the first cello, from Bach's music, conducts him by just looking at him. Nevertheless, it's a fiasco: a demanding public, mediocre acoustics, nil enthusiasm. And someone who doesn't arrive.

During the toast of honor, hidden among the crowd, they drink till they don't know each other anymore and return to the innocence of the beginning. He, a bit more sober, takes her aside and helps her to her room: deliriously, he imagines he can still wash away his pride.

12

I write you this letter though I know you won't read it. Perhaps because of that I dare to defy silence again; for an instant I rejoiced thinking that I would not have to submit again to that torture, that a pen would not be in my hands to pour insipid drops of ink, but I'm incapable of escaping this delirium. I don't understand what absurd mania makes me converse with my own—now worn out—words. I don't oppose any resistance to it, as if it wasn't me but someone else who dictates these lines of pain and blood. My God, how I wish I'd be able to share this with someone—even with you—instead of writing it. Truly, nothing destroys like writing: it annihilates reality instead of preserving it, it immobilizes and exhausts when it attempts to rescue it from oblivion and transience. The sense of the world is found in walking, in movement, in change: it was made only to slide in irrecoverable instants, to be born and die in the blink of an eye. In its place literature, facile remedy of memory, is paralyzed; formed from unsatisfied needs, it doesn't resuscitate anyone. Like love, from its beginning it is doomed to fail. It's a pity I discovered this so late; now, though I know it's useless, that through it I condemn myself, I'm unable to avoid it. I write you because I've decided to hurl myself to the abyss: this way, at least I don't fall into inertia. It will be the only dignified act of my life: to fall off the cliff freely, facing responsibility. Worst of all is that I write you and don't even know you. Did I love you? Whom do we love? Not the individuals themselves, without a doubt, but their images, the nebulous silhouettes we make of them: their residue. In the end—pain proves it—we only exist for those who love us or hate us. Unfortunately, that fearful existence others grant us doesn't resemble our bitterness. That's why the deepest love is the one that has as its object an unknown; that way we possess him without becoming disappointed with the idea we have of him compared to his body. When we live closely with the beloved, when we see him daily, when we are capable of guessing his thoughts, love vanishes and we become aware that the other has been nothing more than a pretext. But it doesn't matter; at this point it's all the same, that you may be an invention of mine and that you may not read this letter: nevertheless, I'll write it for you. Let serendipity test me in this absurd journey, I will test my luck. Very little remains of you: barely a bitter memory, a spasm, never a glance, a word, a caress from you. Everything vanished; not even your name means anything, so, to which of your figures, states of being, feelings, should I address this letter? Which of those eyes, cheeks, tears, insults, are you? I only know that, in spite of the irrationality that goes deep, I love you intensely; my destiny hangs on a single whisper of your lips, on a signal from your hands. That's the paradox: I cannot stop myself from saying nothing to you. Nothing can make me hide that which, because of you and for you, is in me. Nothing can hold me back, not even the fear of hurting you; I hurt you in me, I bleed more than you, I suffer more, but it's necessary. I am possessed this time, nothing in me can negate that which possesses me; I'm possessed by my love for you. It affords me a resolution you are able to see, a lucidity you can feel. I touch you, I see you, I touch you and I see you in me: I am of you, outside of you I'm not myself: let me protect myself from dying. Let me for an instant make myself again out of you; to try it. You know very well how far my violence reached for your mind and for your skin, how much I loved your pain to make it mine, to fill myself with it and free you from its burden. You were an unreachable goal, you fled like your affection; you escaped, fragile with my tears. I followed you even to the mirrors in which you looked at yourself. I'd search for you, I'd trap you, I'd hold you against my breast, only to see how you'd disappear from between my arms. Forgive me if I remind you of it. I've spoken to you; I speak to you with candor, brutally. I've spoken to you in spite of seeing that I hurt you when I speak to you, but I tell you that I hurt myself deeper, that I suffer more horribly and that the worst damage life has dealt me and can still deal me is that I inevitably have to cause you harm, without anything within my power to prevent it, in spite of the fact that everything in me cries upon seeing it and maddens upon feeling it. I'm crying as I have never cried. My whole life is weeping for you. Forgive me; it was I who destroyed you, not time itself. I had to forget you, murder you, and get you out of my head. You and I. And I won: suddenly you no longer mattered to me. I then wanted to extricate the feelings, sinister keys of unwished for doors, apexes of weakness. They would never explain the world to me. I took refuge in intelligence, that cold tumor: with it I constructed a contingent universe, with precise laws, where you were not needed. Chance was forbidden; love proscribed. I lost sight that, even reigning, intelligence always remains alone. Completely alone. Forgive me then, for this letter: I needed to write it and acquire courage for the only possible conclusion, the extreme consequence of my life and my oeuvre. An infinite number of times I repeated that it was important to tear away from the world the scant shreds of truth it shows us: now I see myself compelled to unfasten the most important one, the one that can justify the other ones, the one that can give meaning to tedium and pain, to foolish laughter and punctilious forgetfulness, to your vanished love and to this letter that is lost with my blood.

Beloved, you are present in spite of the dark silence,

Jorge.

13

Going back was even worse than the trip there, surrounded by broken words, violent reproaches, and turbid pauses. I wanted to excuse myself for not having attended the concert, but her stubborn lack of forgiveness made me imperturbable. I could not make her understand the importance of sleeping in that abandoned hovel. Better to resist in silence, delighting in her lack of understanding.

How absurd life becomes with someone else: everything is interpreted; even the most trivial thing is imbued with symbolic value. Impossible to remain in a vacuum: even against my own will silence had expressed it for me. Trapped in my own imperceptible reactions and subject to her winks, her gaze, and her gestures, I understood that those signals were important in and of themselves, hurting us both and even if mistakenly so. I knew it, just one word from her was enough to save me, but neither of us was willing to search for it. We preferred the vanity of the offended one to the gladness of the one showing regret.

In torment, as soon as I arrived in Mexico City I called Eloy. I needed to tell him what was happening with me, with Alma, with Cuesta.

—Who is the victim now?—He asked me upon entering the cafeteria.

—You, as usual—I answered.

But this time I wasn't ready to hear what he had to say, but to talk. I laid out my notes and the first volume of the *Complete Works* by Cuesta on the table, explaining to him my intentions.

—Have you gone mad?

—As much as he did.

Intelligently, he presented innumerable objections, he told me that it wasn't worthwhile to go into that topic, that I ran the risk that what I wrote would be more interesting because of the scandalous nature of the subject matter rather than by virtue of my own conclusions.

—But I'm not looking for my own point of view, I'm looking for Cuesta's—I objected—. What seems incredible to me is that not a single critic has been able to see his oeuvre as an autobiographical document.

Eloy interrupted to order his dinner.

—Do you know the poem "Song to a Mineral God"?

—Yes, he finished it just before he was taken to the mental asylum...

—Precisely—I responded enthusiastically—. And the truth is that, unless it's about something very important, what one thinks least of all, is finishing a poem.

—Unless you've gone mad.

—In my opinion, the end of that poem and the end of Cuesta's life are one and the same. I'm going to write an essay...

He looked at me seriously for some moments, as if he was intuiting my thoughts with those eyes that were able to foretell the bursts of his own poetry.

—It's possible to name another's love and hate—he said, but it's not possible to feel them if we don't repeat them.

Then the conversation digressed into habitual themes, his new collection of poems, his past lovers, and my immobility and, of course, Alma. I could tell him very little then, not even that I could keep her memory clearly in my own mind. We said goodbye, foreseeing the growing distance of our encounters. Nonetheless, throughout the next days I couldn't extricate myself from his conversation. I was sure that I could explore Cuesta to the last consequences, until I could make mine his passions. If I could not rescue my own life, at least I would rescue his.

His name was Jorge, like me, and because of that his life hurt me twice.

SECOND OEUVRE
Vast Deposit of Brief Lives

For desire everything is movement.

URROZ

1

Her obsidian eyes, half-open, scrutinized me from above, lustrous and serene, the shadows contrasting with the paleness of her face and hands, the tenuous dress that covered her. It irritated me; as much of an effort as I'd make to think about something else, to distract my attention from her blind gaze, I couldn't stop feeling like a criminal captured before committing his crime. I wasn't ready to withstand the wait in that cramped hall upholstered in wood and velvet. The seat creaked under my weight and I tried to avoid getting up to leaf through some brochures that had been offered to me, but not even then was I able to rid myself of the sense of oppression. I couldn't resist smoking a cigarette in spite of the silence and cleanliness of that room—and most of all in spite of those black eyes—obstinately forbidding me to do it.

For a moment it occurred to me to finish with the damned sufficiency of the room, to take out a blade, to destroy the papers, the pillows, the staves, and to hollow out those eyes that upset me so, but I immediately accepted my normality. The door of the office opened and Father Rendón appeared. He found me with tense muscles and gaze fixed on that other gaze.

—That's our Lady of Succor—he said, leaning on his cane and pointing to the figure standing before us.

I focused all my rage on the niche but I tried to keep it out of the priest's awareness.

—Sit down—he ordered me, doing likewise, behind an oak desk on which an iron crucifix and a yellowing skull could be seen—.

Coffee?

—No, thank you.

The room fluctuated between a chapel and doctor's office: pictures of Jesus and the pope next to abundant anatomical diagrams. In the center, encased in a brown frame, a doctor's diploma granted by the National University. Definitely, Father Rendón didn't hide his double character as scientist and religious man; in fact he seemed to highlight it at any opportunity, with scarce Christian modesty.

—It seems I didn't understand you this morning. What exactly do you want from us?—his energetic voice neared sweetness.

—Pardon me, Father—I began—. I am working on a study about Cuesta, a poet who was a patient here during the forties. I would like to know about his mental state, how he behaved, who came to visit him, are there any files...?

—Are you a relative of his?

—No, no. As I told you, I am a researcher and I'm writing about him.

From behind his glasses his expression was distant, immovable. He caressed his whitening eyebrows and mumbled in a tone that this time was coming from the clergyman in him:

—Then we can't do anything for you.

—But father, you haven't understood: he spent his last days here, this is very important.

—You're the one who doesn't understand—he took off his glasses, carefully folded them and placed them on the table—. I'm sorry, it's impossible to offer you our help. There is a rule to destroy patient's files twenty years after their death. That was…

—In 1942.

—Do you see? It doesn't depend on us.

—Wouldn't there be someone who still remains from those years, someone who may have known him then?

—As you know, the hospital was under different ownership. None of us was here.

—And among the patients?

—I don't know, perhaps.

—Can you investigate?

Repentant, he sent me to Dr. Galindo, who would be in charge of helping find an answer. A recent graduate, she was a young and beautiful woman, with the affable smile of a doctor who still feels beyond pain. While she led me through interminable hallways, she spoke about her job, her interaction with the patients and that other state of consciousness we aren't able to glimpse in them. She chatted freely, without allowing me a word edgewise —I only wanted to know if someone would be able to help me—, while explaining to me her perspective on madness.

Her optimistic view seemed to vanish in the aseptic desolation of the place: green and red tiles repeated themselves like mirrors, the chrome of the bars and walking aids, and the lamps and images on the walls didn't show a speck of dust, of impurity. Even so, the general impression was one of emptiness, as if the authorities of the institution wished that their people would not be contaminated by the world outside.

A Magic Mountain upside down: the sanatorium as a refuge against the malignancy from outside.

At last we went into the patio and the doctor led me toward a large garden of hedges and bushes with a fountain in the middle. There were just two or three trees, and in spite of the extreme care and the artificial beauty of the roses, the sight of very high walls wouldn't allow for any other thought than that of enclosure.

—Madmen are strangled poets—she said, not citing anyone, as a warning to my complacency.

I almost hadn't been able to tell her of my project, and doubted that she'd ever heard of Cuesta, but her peroration seemed to be formulated specifically for him. The doctor would tear away the grandiloquence of her patients, those languid bodies chasing each other in an impossible race around the patio.

Circling the fountain, dozens of patients, decked in gray dress, marched slowly inside an imaginary merry go-round. Nothing obligated them to it, though it was difficult not to think of a non-existent foreman, a fury, an infinite sadness.

—Why do they walk in circles? —I asked the doctor.

She ventured various hypotheses, got tangled in several speculations not wanting to commit to anyone in particular—

her plurality as a psychiatrist—, but the last thing she said, a remark to which she attributed minimal importance, impressed me with the force of a revelation:

—Perhaps they want to exit time.

2

Outside of time, outside of reason. Their weakness, to give it a sort of name, consisted in stealing themselves from the continuous process of change: that's where their madness, their rebellion lay. Not strangled poets, but fugitive poets that favored a clandestine existence rather than submit themselves to the absurd rules of time. This anomaly, this anti-normality, could be read in the liquid depth of their pupils, in the muddy bed of their iris, where the gaze that sinks further toward the interior of their old bodies can be guessed. Nobody remembered his, diluted in the humidity of the building; the patients and even the doctors called him Spider. They'd say it was dangerous to speak with him, that his skin was sticky and his saliva poisonous. The inmates had invented for him—or attached to him—a story.

They'd say that Spider had killed his wife during an inexplicable bout of anger. That he'd strangled her and then hung her from a tree. When the police captured him, he was brutally beaten; the cops asked time and again why he'd done it, but Spider refused to speak. He mumbled that no one would be able to understand him: he had saved her with his own condemnation, with his own sacrifice. When it became useless to vex him any longer, he was taken to the insane asylum; he wasn't expected to survive.

Nevertheless, fifty years later, Spider remained in the same place, excluded from a world that no longer preserved any witness of his guilt.

Contrary to what was whispered, as if he was able to cloak the past, he had the face of a frail and innocent child, enveloped by graying hair and wrinkles as if they were part of a mask.

Doctor Galindo respectfully introduced him to me: he was a monument, a serene guardian of shadows. His little white eyes—he suffered of almost total blindness—emanated a tenuous luminosity.

—Spider—she said, leaning on his back—this man wants to chat with you. Tell him about your earlier years here, of the time of your arrival. Do you understand?

Spider nodded; who knows when it was last that anyone visited him. The doctor left us alone, he asked me to follow him to his room; he held on to the railing and we began a slow walk.

I asked about his nickname and he answered that Spider was his real name; he said things are called based on their qualities and that he, ever since arriving at the hospital, had taken up weaving a wicker carpet; that he was determined to dedicate the rest of his life to this endeavor, and that it was logical thereof, that his name be Spider.

—Why a carpet?—I asked him, sitting on his bed.

—Because in it are the causes of destiny and of salvation, the escape of the soul from the abyss of hell, the motive to liberate ourselves from sin and from the devil but most of all from the sins of the devil and from the hell of sense and from the destiny of the soul.—His voice slid monotonous and sweet—. I have to assemble with my fingers the knots of my former days, don't I?

There wasn't a trace of the gigantic woven piece anywhere, but I comprehended something in his obsession: a desire to rewrite his past, to reorganize it.

—Why weave without stopping?

—Time doesn't stop but moves on; the image dies, yes, it aspires to that which passes.

I couldn't keep his attention even for an instant; his thoughts would fall over a cliff without course. What to do with someone who dies and resuscitates each moment?

—And why a carpet?—I inquired.

—Too many whys without reason, right?

I was ashamed.

—Listen, I don't know if you can remember him, it has been some time, in '42... A man, a poet who was here before committing suicide... Cuesta, his last name was Cuesta.

—What was the color of his eyes?

—Mm, green, I think—I responded—. One lowered eyelid.

He took his time answering, interlaced his hands.

—Yes, yes, I remember them, very green in dark skin, with flames in his hair, right? I remember well; ugly, right?

—What I'd like you to tell me...

—Life is vain, profound and sad—he interrupted angrily, on the brink of tears—. I keep him with me, poor him. A woman used to visit him. Very sad, isn't it?

—Are you sure it was him, Jorge Cuesta, the poet?

—It leaves my blindness behind, the image that retires. As soon as I discover him, he disappears. Can't you see that I can't name him?—His white eyes became bloodshot, he was trembling—. Can't you see it's impossible to get to know anyone else? It's not to be attempted nor pursued. Nothing of that or this; nothing, nothing. All that remains to oneself is to weave alone, to escape alone, to sleep alone, to eat alone, to dream alone, and to live alone...

A strong bout of coughing made him fall on the floor, his skin seemed to break apart, he spit. He reddened as if he were to explode, the body full of diminutive mustard seeds. I got up to call Dr. Galindo, but the old man grasped my arm with clammy, sticky fingers.

—No—he gasped—. My health is fine, I'm going to die but my health is fine—and he laughed grotesquely—. I assure you, truly: the rest is silence. And a wicker carpet.

Perhaps he never met Cuesta, perhaps he confused him with someone else, deceived me, but I listened to him as if his words were the only certitude of my life.

3

I don't know what happened to us, truly I don't know. Because the reality is, the only real thing is that we stopped getting to know each other. There's no longer a bond to link us. But understand this, it isn't that Jorge and I may be incapable of communicating with each other or that we may be unable to solve our problems; none of that. The two of us are ready to enter into a dialogue and accustomed to escape together from that which bothers us. Totally the opposite: our faults, if we must give them a name, don't lie in what we say, rather in what we keep silent.

It's been some time, I don't know how long, that I feel far from him; his acts, his omissions, everything he does seems unclear, and I suppose that the same happens to him with regard to myself. A relationship cannot be sustained with an infinite number of more or less pacific discussions; words, with their nooks and labyrinths, get enclosed, explode, and then become diluted into lesser themes.

I remember that at the beginning I was sure about him just by looking at him, and I'm not referring to his muteness, but to a deeper presentment concerning his way of looking at things. Instead, now I observe him: the signs remain constant, but lack meaning. As if they'd been emptied. Why does he behave like that? What do I mean to him? This absence hurts me, though in fact it shows a worse detachment: what hurts me is the idea that it ought to hurt me and it doesn't. I don't know if I love him or if I hate him. If at least I were able to discover what keeps us apart...

I imagine that his purpose is to keep watch over me and to bewilder me, but that trick is too simple for him: he agreed to remain together with the sole desire in mind of ignoring me, doubly jealous from the effort of not wanting that it be so. Tortuously incorrigible, he pretends to show his sufficiency without abandoning me. It's a stupid game he thinks he'll win when he knows his defeat from the beginning. His own dignity cornered me in a decision that turned out unjust for both of us: to leave the rules alone or carry them out to their last consequences.

You know what happened afterward. But I repeat to you that I never lost my lucidity, not for an instant did I cease to understand what I was doing or why I was doing it, believe me. But I don't feel badly vis a vis Jorge, it was also his fault. Though, what can be the importance of all this to you?

4

Immortality in an instant. That was his goal throughout his life and his oeuvre, his passion. Immortality that knows what it means to step outside of time, to drag it, to dilate it till all seconds fit into one. From alchemy to modern chemistry, from the philosopher's stone to the synthesis of hormones, the obsession is unique: the pleasure that doesn't last, transformed into a constant flux, well beyond days. An adventure of decades that culminated in the potions that he himself prepared and self-administered, attempting to modify his body, by then in full-blown schizophrenic overflows, but that began much earlier, with impeccable judgment during his university years. Then, when no one had imagined his madness, the distressing justifications that he wrote to Doctor Gonzalo Lafora (published by Miguel Capistrán in *Vuelta*, May of 1977), or his sexual deliriums, Cuesta wrote his bachelor's thesis: *Process for the Synthetic Production of Enzymatic Substances with Specific Attitude and their Applications.*

When at last I found the biochemistry section, after walking the full length of the National Library from one end to the other, it made sense that it would be empty. Hiding in a hall to which access was only possible through a narrow corridor on the fourth floor, it seemed to be safe from any reader.

Sitting behind a stack of books, a man whose face leaned a few centimeters away from his desk, drew on a piece of paper, avoiding the ensuing tedium of the place. His attitude was understandable: what else could he do but kill time (even at the risk of committing suicide slowly) in such a job.

I walked toward the counter, waited a moment, coughed, waited again, and already exasperated, requested his attention in a loud voice. He got up from his chair, unwrinkled his overcoat with the initials of the university, abandoned his pen and addressed me with his face tainted with the stain of boredom.

—Good morning —I said.

—Morning.

He took his handkerchief from his pocket, extended it on the palm of his hand and blew his nose; he then folded it into four sides, made it into a rhomboid shape and placed it back on his front pocket.

—I'm looking for a very rare work —I began to say and handed over to him the small piece of paper in which I'd jotted the information.

—Look it up over there, on the left hand side cabinet —he responded as if he'd been obligated to say the most obvious thing in the world.

On the other side of the reading area there was an opaque collection of metallic cabinets. I began to look at the drawers first, attempting to find the title, then the author or the subject, but without result. Nothing about enzymes or any such thing. The awful disorder the cards were in, prevented any attempt at finding anything; it was as if no one had paid any attention to them in years. I felt myself observed, followed, tricked. I walked back to the counter, insulting the clerk in silence.

—I'm sorry —I told him with defeated serenity—, but not only do I not find what I need, there isn't even a subject heading resembling it. How is that possible?

—Did you look into the catalogue by subject matter?

I sensed him enjoying my failure behind his bulky manner. As if the order of the world, represented by that individual, were denied to me deliberately.

—Yes, there aren't enzymes, nor enzymatic substances nor hormones, or anything like it.

He stood up with difficulty, advanced toward me dragging his fleshy self and ended with his head right next to my face. His sour breath hit me. I wanted to strike him.

—Show me the paper one more time.

He looked at it. I couldn't stand his condescending tone, the perspiration on his temples, his nervous fingers pointing at me.

—If it's a professional thesis, why don't you look for it in the School of Chemistry —he was talking to me as if I was a lost student.

—They don't preserve anything from those years: 1926.

I had a horrible headache, felt dizzy, almost ready to explode. If I could, I would have killed him.

—Can I give you some advice? —he said irritated—. Try and find it with his relatives. Relatives always keep those kinds of things even if they're not of any use to them. When my sister received her degree in Psychology…

I didn't find out anything else.

5

—What's the true difference between a man and a woman?—I asked ruminating innumerable times upon that question.

Her eyes shined with green intensity, barely distracted from her chore revising musical scores.

—What are you talking about?—she responded.

Sitting in a kitchen chair she labored, noting the arcades to Bruckner's Seventh.

—Yes, what do you think may be the real difference between men and women? What makes us such opposites?

She left the pencil on the table, raised her face in a cynical way and directed an obscene gesture toward me.

—So what did you think?—and returned to the analysis of the music.

Only then did I look at her: a body, not a voice, which was exposed with the sole intention of being denied to me. She didn't have a trace of make-up on her face and wore her hair tied with a ribbon; a t-shirt that could barely be described as white and a thin black skirt revealed the precise forms of her skin. Her bare feet didn't even brush the floor tile; supporting each other, they caressed themselves with enjoyment. Seldom had I ever seen her look so beautiful: it was a shame that such opaque sensuality would be wasted in the chore she was carrying out. I didn't resist the temptation of caressing her neck, leaning softly over the musical staves, but with a brusque movement made to look spontaneous, she moved away from my hands.

—You haven't answered—I defended myself—. What makes you and me so different? Nature's genetics and nothing else?—She didn't pay any attention, I continued talking—. I'm going to put it to you another way: Are our souls alike? Or are they separate halves, like our bodies? If, for example, a man were to take suddenly the body of a woman, could you continue loving him as a man?

Her expression contorted violently, she pushed away the musical scores and turned toward me.

—A man is a man and a woman is a woman in every-thing—and she underlined the last word.

She moved back the chair and sat on it in a strange lotus position, with crossed legs. Unconsciously she caressed her small, white feet.

How brilliant—I said—. No, what I ask is if our essences are similar or if, like our bodies, they only complement each other and therefore remain incomplete.

—Both—annoyed she arranged her skirt playing with her ankles—. Why are you talking to me about this?

—Damn it! I don't make myself clear. Let's see. You and I desire each other because my body is that of a man and yours is of a woman, right? Well, what would happen if your body turned into that of a man and mine into that of a woman? Would we still love each other?

—That's stupid. I don't want to hear any more.

—Wait—I held her arm and burned myself upon touching her—. I'm not talking about homosexuality, but about the interior self.

—You're crazy.

She changed her posture, sat straight with her knees together and crossed her arms; her hands pressed delicately upon the spheres of her breasts, delineated through the pleats of her shirt.

—Enough!—I could feel the pain of my hot body inside my pants—. I want to know what would happen if our organisms were modified, if suddenly we were able to have the opposite sex or if...

—What?

—If we could have both sexes.

Jumping, she stood up, her muscles contracting in a type of anticipated shame. Her disheveled hair fell unevenly over her shoulders. Her smell intoxicated me.

—What's the matter with you?—Her eyelids moistened.

—I held her strongly, enjoying the contact. I looked at her, drawing my lips close to hers as if I wished to drink her shortness of breath.

—Imagine it—I could only think of biting her—, try and imagine it without prejudice: with both sexes pleasure would be immense; to fill and be filled, I in your body and you in mine.

I could almost touch her with my tongue, feeling her breasts open toward me, her shirt damp with my breath.

—Just think about it—I repeated, holding her—. Cuesta

believed that in something like that he would find perfection, immortality. —Her pupils distilled terror. —An eternal, interminable orgasm...

I brushed my hand against her cheek, then over her nape and neck until bordering one of her nipples and her belly.

—You're crazy—she said—. I'm telling you you're crazy—. She left. Mute and in disbelief I remained in the kitchen,
thinking about how little she understood me, of how much I
desired her, about the sad dryness of our union.

6

Again I find myself here, subject to the anguish of what is unpredictable; pouring out the last drop on these pages any of my remaining lucidity. I regret it, I broke my promise, the pain got the best of me; I need to say it, shout it, even if no one hears, even if no one understands, not even you. Doubly risky situation: on the one hand I die, on the other I have the secret sense of having succeeded. As if nevertheless, at the end of the road, there was an ultimate out, a chink to escape weeping, but also, and before it, the possibility of finding the highest cliff. I must preserve the scant objectivity that still remains before I completely turn into dust, clay, flame. I know there's very little time left, I sense it, and foresee the niches of my soul. That is why I write you now and rescue from the cobweb of my senses a few impressions that may permit me to unstring the story line of my last days. Help me; I can't stand it any longer. Near, very near. Nevertheless, it is upon touching the fire that we burn ourselves, not while remaining at its center. At this moment, I am pain, disenchantment, agony; while I'm unable to cross the thin barrier that separates me from salvation I will be consumed in the worst of all punishments: uncertainty. I don't understand where I'm headed, which path I've taken, though having come this far it's not possible to turn back. Not until I succeed or fail will I be able to know if I've wasted my intelligence and my life or if it has not been in vain. It is there, hard and yet, I don't come out of it as yet. It's tepid, bland, and extensive. I don't cease to touch it, I don't cease to preserve it if I open my eyes, if

I close them, if I speak or if I remain silent; if I lay down, if I sit or if I walk; if I hear the outside sounds or if I hear only a pleasant buzz. It penetrates everything, it invades it all; it is in all parts of the air, even in the deepest of them; in everything that I see and touch and in everything that touches me and looks at me. What superficial, and physical languidness, linked with such internal and profound agility. It is a liberating silent voluptuousness that has the power to suppress contradictions, tie opposites. The mystery that I own. Reconciling the opposites of heaven and earth I take myself away from the design that wounds everything, that blots everything, that consumes it all.

Reintegrating what is dispersed, chaos, the process of change is defied, that dark corruptor of angels. The answer is to be found in the wound itself that has hurled us into time. It is the cause of our submersion in this daily death that loneliness makes us confuse with life. Nothing more distant: ours is a constant degradation, slow putrefaction, and aging. No, life is far from being an infinite succession of instants. The only way to escape time isn't through trying to eliminate it, nor trying to annihilate the hours or drilling down to our image of the present. On the contrary, the way to do it is through joining the opposites, reweaving the distanced balls of yarn…the antipodes are nullified, the extremes neutralized. To this end I've dedicated my days; as if man and the universe were no more than a vessel shaped by God that we have managed to break, I've decided to be the one to repair His creation: to be His artisan. The mission hasn't been finished, but as soon as I complete it the disrupted order will be restored; I will find serenity, contemplation, and equilibrium. That's why I'm telling you I'm about to triumph. I see that which prolongs in time this sensation of life and everything I have is charged with all I will have. I see it, I can almost touch it. I believe I won't be able to contain it and it comes more and more though I may close my eyes and not see anything; though I may become distracted with what I see and touch; though I may forget everything I feel. In nothingness it makes itself present and penetrates me. In the most strange, in the worst enemy, the same happiness I find that which dilates. May dense silence swallow the black, obscure rumor.

Beloved, you are present in spite of the dark silence,

Jorge.

7

In the office that morning I presented my resignation letter. I couldn't continue any longer in that voluntary prison. Upon finding out, Alma went berserk as if I'd addressed her with the harshest insult. Worse than Cuesta. Or was it possible he also had something to do with this? Yes, in some way. But in the end I was doing it for her, to preserve some of my love for her: more than a defiant act, it was proof of my affection. I needed her more than ever, though I felt incapable of telling her, of imploring her acquiescence.

Lonely, terrifyingly lonely, I phoned Natalia, the poet's sister, to ask her about the professional thesis. She herself answered affably, telling me that she had shown it to Louis Panabière, and that she would gladly make it available to me the same day, during a two hour period in her library. She urged me to be punctual and knock only once on the door. Then, she continued, a maid would lead me to the room where I could study the document till ten in the evening. There wouldn't be any other contact, word or greeting; no other sign from the woman who perhaps was the only person capable of telling me something truly important about the poet.

On the coffee table appeared the crumpled volume. I sat down, took out a notebook from my portfolio and got ready to examine the yellowing bundle of papers, to unearth the possible roots of his poetry.

During the two hours I reviewed the formulas, drafted some descriptions —I could hardly understand anything— and wanted to imagine the processes being expounded on, but deep inside I knew that the extravagant mechanisms contained there were useful to me only as evidence of his obsession. It was like reading a biography of the "Song," the rough scaffolding of its changes and metamorphoses. Transits, displacements and jumps that showed the precociousness of his demons, the fatidic dénouement announced in chemistry's neutrality.

But more important than the substances, hatchings, and mixes, was the loose page I found intermingled with the last pages of the text. It was a piece of wrapping paper showing awkward and blurred handwriting; with a different type of ink —perhaps Natalia's— the date had been recorded: August, 1942. That night would have been worth it, only to know of his unhinged sadness. Since then I keep it sealed in my memory:

In the everlasting Samarkand
urges an extenuate candy twirin
the streptococci of a burin
with marvelous gildings of saraband.

My warm peduncle trips
over the raggedy numid of organdips.

8

In March, the magazine *Plural* published part of my preliminary study, an essay titled *The Magisterium of Jorge Cuesta*. I wrote:

During the last four years of his life, Cuesta had two main concerns essentially —though for me it is one with two aspects—on one hand the series of experiments started in 1932 to synthesize enzymes and, in the end, stop the passage of time; and on the other, the writing of the "Song to a Mineral God." Repeatedly, the relation between the two endeavors has been pointed out, the harmony of Cuesta the chemist —or alchemist— with Cuesta the poet, but the commentaries have never been devoid of skepticism. In most of them, Cuesta only makes use of hermetic symbolism to enrich his literature; sometimes capricious, undecipherable at times, the alchemical images have barely any value. On the contrary, almost no one has wanted to realize that the "Song" is more than a poem about the states and transformations of inert matter, as has been stated by Salvador Elizondo; on the contrary, the "Song" is the summary of a lifetime, of its quest and also —it must be said— of a death. It is not a question of finding in his madness and suicide the cause of his poetry, but finding in the latter, in his idea of the world, the cause of his tragic end.

In response to his critics, I will say that in Cuesta the opposite of what they say is what happens: in all of his work, as a chemist and as a poet, one notes the same, and let's be clear, only interest in Alchemy: the desire to reach permanence, to avoid fugacity, to become the master of time. In fact, the phi-losopher's stone, the goal of alchemists serves to prepare the panacea or universal cure which is the elixir of a long life. The attainment of what is fixed through that which is volatile, the attainment of what's permanent through that which is transi-tory, thanks to the reconciling of opposites, that is the object of the Alchemical Work, none other.

Nigel Grant Sylvester states that information from various sources suggests that halfway through the decade of the thirties, Cuesta was experimenting with chemical formulas and was ob-sessed with the idea of discovering the elixir of life, the panacea for all illnesses...It is rumored that he invented a method to refine waste oil from combustion engines, a formula to make wine, another one to induce a quick process of fermentation in natural wines; that he discovered a liquid of which only a few drops were necessary to counteract the intoxication produced by the strongest alcoholic drinks, and a pill to preserve energy during sustained periods of time. One of the stories most fre-quently told is the one about his experiments with enzyme reac-tions and that he had invented a process to suspend the ripening of fruits (*Life and Works of Jorge Cuesta*).

In all these inventions —in the double meaning of the term— Cuesta's obsession with the passage of time is mani-fest, and furthermore, with finding a way to create sensations and things —specifically pleasure— durable and permanent. The best example of that is his substance to delay the ripening of oranges: a miniature sample of the powers of the philoso-pher's stone. Additionally, the hormones that he self-adminis-tered, according to his letter to Doctor Lafora, produced real anatomical modifications in his body, to transform him into a hermaphrodite, the alchemical rebus formed by uniting the opposites. Defying other specialists, it occurs to me that Cuesta really suffered those morphological changes he mentioned: in the end Doctor Lafora never carried out a physical examination before his diagnosis of repressed homosexuality. In any case, true or false, the important thing is the poet's vision, completely lucid and only attributable to a conscious state of supreme clarity. Cuesta was convinced that through reintegrating the sexual duality of man, it would be possible to escape time and achieve immortality. That is the fruit of which time is owner, as he says in the last verses of his "Song." I'm truly convinced that Cuesta's work isn't that of a deranged individual, but of a visionary, and also, as I will refer in subsequent works, that his theories are verifiable in this day and age.

The following month, in a letter to the editor, the first in a long list of responses to my essay appeared. It was signed by Igor Padilla who, after an unending string of insults, ended it saying: How is it possible that a study so lacking in seriousness could be published? The ignorance of the author is surprising, the quantity of prejudices, but most of all, the irresponsibility in dealing with medical and psychological topics the author has not even bothered to corroborate. It's terrible to see such lack of scruples, etcetera, etcetera.

But it was an article writer from *Novedades* newspaper that lit the flame of a great —and for me unthought-of— fire of invectives and envies. I was accused of being an arriviste, of twisting the story however way I pleased, of seeking to scandalize, of citing out of context and of wanting nothing but ill-conceived fame. But the worst overreach —the article concluded— occurs when he pretends to become the sole inheritor of the

Cuestian tradition. Without any basis or a revelatory discovery, he dares to say that Cuesta wasn't crazy—of course not, we are the ones who are crazy— and that he was reasonable in his alchemical inventions. I don't know how the author of the essay will substantiate the validity of his arguments, as he tells us, but he will now have to do so.

Soon similar replies appeared everywhere, with titles such as *Who Owns the Truth about Cuesta?*, *A Theory That Isn't Worth That which It Costs or Coasts Downhill*. They'd refer to me with adjectives that ranged from being labeled a charlatan to being called a repressed homosexual (the paradox, had it not been so acid, would have amused me). It was more than I was able to tolerate. Perhaps my speculations sounded absurd, but just because of that, as the writer from *Novedades* had ascertained, I was ready to prove them.

—There you have the seriousness of your work— Alma reproached me.

Then she apologized, but the damage was already done. What remained of me at the end of all that rigmarole? Not much.

9

—I must tell you about it —she tells him—. I don't know why, but I have to do it.

Their erratic and out of breath voices, speak in spite of themselves, by necessity, as if they didn't want to hear their words nor understand them, following the sound of their desolation.

—It's Jorge again —she begins—. Why is it so difficult to love somebody?

She caresses her own forehead, she is trembling.

—I'm sorry, for the first time I realize I love him. I love Jorge yet I cannot be with him, it disgusts me to see him, his stupid pride. But I truly love him and I can't help it.

Disconnected pieces torn from her memory, glimpses of her passion, are inscribed in her head. How to value them in an instant? She is not able to comprehend yet what he has meant for her. She despairs, it hurts her to be there, conversing with another man, telling him about her anguish as if it was nothing, but destiny has converted the subject it disdains in the receptacle of its open wounds.

—Why do you insist on this? —he says.

She guesses the answer, has known it from the beginning. She prefers to stop talking and get angry.

—If it doesn't interest you I can leave —she says—. Can't you see what it means?

—An act of confession? —he says, almost playfully.

He turns and observes her under the projected shadows of her face trying to discover what lies behind the intermittent and empty story that has brought them together.

—He didn't matter to me at the beginning, it's true —she continues—. Not even when I broke up with you. It was the type of company that slowly became inevitable...I got used to his presence.

—Is that why you are still with him?

—At the time I didn't have anyone else. Now it's different.

—Did you want to take revenge with me, to show me your indifference?

—You don't understand: he always loved me.

—And is that enough? Do you think that speaks in your favor?

—Of course not —she says—. But in the end it turned out stronger than my hatred. It's very strange, now, when I know I love him, I've lost him.

The man, annoyed, has no appetite for that clumsy conversation on the reaches of love. He gives her a deep and acid kiss and the two of them wrap themselves again within the sheets. He embraces her breasts, coldly molds her nipples with sleep; she barely gets excited, presses her thighs against the hips of the other, kisses his neck, and cheek, and belly, but not his lips, never again. Lapses of fury submit once again to the ritual. They pant, bite each other, and contort their bodies: they fight more than enjoy each other. He grasps her, penetrates her flesh, sinking and emptying himself into her.

In the end they separate without realizing they're doing so and lie in opposite sides of the bed. She thinks: love is not what holds us here. The man stands up and with a soft voice that in fact is an order —the only one he can give her, the only one she can obey— he indicates:

—Leave him.

She weeps and says yes.

10

The gestures of the faces don't show the least trace of piety; their devastated smile is the only thing that remains in a countenance full of sarcasm. The black eyes, stabbing, distill unbelievable hatred. Unfolding, the lips color of blood, open about to burst. They are monsters, gods, mirages. The hands, yes, of creators, light and turbid, languid Renaissance hands. Even demons need these sublimely human instruments to become evident in the world, be profligate with others' lives and attain eternal sentences. Then the fingers appear: they sustain on a tray where moonlight reflects on their bodies, a torso with two heads. On the metallic plate rests, decapitated, a man's head. The features are recognizable: one executioner is Lupe, implacable demiurge, the other is his sister; the victim is Cuesta the poet.

Disgusted, I hurled the book on the table; I felt like throwing up. I went to the bathroom but nothing came out. My head burned, also my neck, and throat. My brain wasn't able to escape the images of those drawings. How were they capable of doing that? Why did she do it? How extensive was her anger, to ask Rivera for that cover and publish it as part of her novel, the hypocritical autobiography that she didn't dare call by its name?

The poet met Lupe Marín, the author of *The Only One*, at a salon: he never imagined where that initial conversation would lead. I see him sitting there, waving his long fingers, stealing time to monopolize the attention of his hostess. He makes an impression with his measured tone of voice, his intelligence and firmness; he tells her he is about to travel to Europe, where he will be an initiate like other Latin American artists, but as soon as he returns he will look her up. She tells him that she doubts it.

I return to his image later, in a Parisian room in the Suez Hotel, Boulevard St. Michel 31, regretting the trip, locked up in cold loneliness, I catch a glimpse of the ice that will follow after him always. He can only think of going back to her: he still thinks himself capable of living a normal existence. A Dutch ship —new paradox— returns him to Mexico, to Lupe's arms, to the disappointment of Lupe, to the frustration of Lupe, the hatred of Lupe, the final abandonment of Lupe. Four years disappear leaving as their only byproduct the worst of sins: Jorge becomes a father. Lupe returns to Rivera, the chimerical whale who dismissed her before: she writes *The Only One* and asks the painter for a few sketches to assassinate the poet.

Alone, Cuesta cloisters himself in his laboratory. I see him hungry, without shaving, marked by conscience's dark circles under the eyes. He takes advantage of his position in the Society of Alcohol Producers to obtain the substances for the Work. He manipulates the elements carefully, protects the fire with his own life, following with great care the chain of the most minimal events that conform his art. The metamorphoses occurring inside the vessels —and within his very flesh— replicate universal recipes, the primordial mechanisms of creation. Fermentations, dilutions, coagulations, take place one after the other in the heat of the oven and his pen. Simultaneous processes: heaven, earth, the Work, man. It's also the rebus, the face that adventurously leans over the sleepy water of a mirror.

Astonished, he finally observes the vessel and the poem that summarizes the transmutation.

The "Song" announces the chemical triumph. Without thinking about it too much, the poet takes a mortar and grinds the scarlet grains that have resulted from the experiment; he adds an excipient and prepares the solution that he then introduces into the tube of a syringe. Enzymes? Elixir? The philosopher's stone? His own body as test field, guinea-pig, self-sacrifice. He faces the risk: to bet everything in a last act which is his poetry. His physiological and organic conversion, his androgynous mutation, is the banal, external appearance, the mask of the secret. Instead, inside awaits the eternal. Immortality is to remain there, contemplating yourself without being able to do anything else other than to look at yourself. Immortality like a mirror.

Suddenly, in an instant, in darkening shadows, he realizes his mistake. And weeps and shouts and despairs and goes mad. That is not the path: it must be traveled in reverse.

In reverse, my God. In the bathroom of my house, my face on the toilet, spitting, I also realize the mistake. And I weep, and shout, and despair, and go mad.

11

I can't take it anymore. And he is there as usual, next to me, ready to torture me, defeat me. Memory oppresses the opaque memory that darkens. Exhausted, I become his victim. He has me, he carries me along, and he leads me. I'm not capable of struggling against him. He permits me everything, even the lowest, ennobling it.

I went out of the house. It rained.

12

Ten in the evening. The place seemed to be empty, the front lights turned off, silence, no one moving inside. I felt my body about to shatter, excited by the absurd peace that had followed upon the tails of the storm. The wind beating on my back burned me instead of wounding me. Everywhere I turned I saw my face reflected in puddles of water, distorted by the ripples swaying on their surface: my features under that terse atmosphere refused to be mine.

I put the key inside and went in. In the distance—a whisper, an invitation—I could hear the pricking sound of a shower; a tenuous glow emanating from the bathroom drew the awkward silhouettes of furniture and curtains. I turned on the light; I discovered a dirty ashtray on the coffee table and quickly returned the room to darkness. I poured myself a brandy: the alcohol warmed my blood. I could smell my own sweat dripping from my armpits and my sides, pooling in my belly. I made an effort to calm down, but an idea began to take hold of my lucidity: an atrocious image enveloped me and was wearing me out...impulsively I wanted to call a doctor, or anyone who could help me. In vain, thirst and desire seemed to grow by the minute.

Desperately I ran to the bedroom, turned on the lamp and lay on the bed. The weight of those days, the suffering and the fever tortured my temples, destroyed me with a cruel and obscene delirium. I needed my hands to calm me down. I began to rub my nape, my shoulders; I unbuttoned my shirt and pants and implacably caressed my chest till reaching my inner thighs, till reaching my sex, holding it, molding it, imagining its pleasures, and lastly letting go of it brusquely. I got up, opened Alma's drawer: perfumes, boxes, papers, cheap jewels and medicines; afterwards lipstick, eye shadows, eye-liners, mascara, pencils, brushes, facial powder: everything ready to be used. I took off my shirt, brought closer the dresser's mirror, and ecstatically debased, I surrendered to the power of those masks.

Certain that Alma still remained in the shower I slipped into the bathroom. Behind the thin blue curtain it was possible to notice her shadow enveloped in steam; her blurry movements were subtle laceration on the cloth. For an instant I contemplated her scrubbing her thighs and covered with foam before violently opening the curtain and exposing her to me. Nude, vulnerable, she couldn't conceive she was watching me. The humidity had made trickles of the paint on my face, black and red, and violet ulcers dripped on my cheeks toward deeply red lips.

She snatched the towel from the coat rack and wrapped herself in it. With her eyes half-closed, still soapy, she exclaimed what have you done, and tried to flee. Why, she shouted, avoiding me, why are you doing this? I let her talk, allowing her to come into the hallway, but nothing more. You've gone crazy, Jorge, please, and I grasped her arm, Jorge, for the last time, it seemed as if in spite of her revulsion she wished to caress me, crying, as if trying to clean it forever, Jorge.

Too late. I took her by the wrists and hitting her all at once, she fell on the floor. She had to understand one way or another. Her poor wet body, barely covered, curled into a ball that I stained with make-up. I love you, you don't understand how much I love you, I told her. She wept, she opened her eyes, as if she wished to trap me in her gaze, a last Jorge nailed in her pupils, and closed them definitively for the night. I tore away the towel and without putting up any resistance she surrendered her mute, empty skin to me.

Without a moan or a shout, not even a word. Nothing. As if I didn't exist, as if I had not been there.

13

—I still don't understand what is it you were trying to accomplish.

Eloy's pupils shone intensely, moistened by a fear that couldn't be settled.

—I still don't believe it—his voice attempted to sound understanding.

—I had to make her see that I'm right—I answered.

—The only thing you proved is that you need help.

His words hurt. But who else could offer me solace?

—I didn't want to hurt her—it was a thread in my thoughts—. I only wanted her to understand...

There wasn't a phrase capable of expressing my ideas; language had not been made to speak about such pain.

—Now she's gone—my voice faltered—, forever.

—You must talk to her—he lied.

—It's not worth it, it was necessary that we separate. It's better, perhaps.

Suddenly I felt he couldn't help me any longer.

—You know something?—I said—. I know what I did to her was terrible, but at bottom I'm unable to regret it. I am a wandering without sense.

—No, you're an imbecile. You must put an end to this, and right away.

I laughed at his obvious stupidity.

—Let's go, please—I insisted.

He paid the check and went outside. I wanted to leave but he made me walk alongside him for several blocks. An abyss of people swarmed from one place to the other under midday's heat.

—Everything repeats itself—I said without thinking.

In his head it continued floating unsustainably, the image of his friend.

—Damn it, I'm not talking about the eternal return—I continued—, but of those moments when by chance, two lives begin to tangle up with each other.

—Do you think that's what happened to you?

—Perhaps. But Cuesta also has a preceding echo: Nietzsche. Madness, death, the sisters, absolute intelligence...

—And you therefore think you must imitate them.

—I'm sorry, it's too late—I leaned on his shoulder as if it was I who needed to cheer him up—. My life doesn't have any other meaning than to try this path. I don't know where it will lead, nor does it matter to me, but it's mine. That's what remains as my sole salvation.

—To save yourself? From what?

Finally a cloud covered the sun momentarily. Time stood still, a crack in the world had opened and I was flung down toward its center.

THIRD OEUVRE
The Taste of Darkness

And nothing remains but the impious joy
of reason falling into the ineffable
and glacial intimacy of its emptiness

PAZ

1

To sink, to know the worst abysses, to debase oneself into extreme corruption. Only then, from affliction covered in mud, it's possible that a last occasion for triumph may open. The taste of darkness is the only sense of immortality and of the future. In this way, upon delineating the last strophes of the poem, Cuesta was drafting his testament and instilling into whatever he was going to be doing from then on, a new lustrous, exhausting light.

It occurred to me to travel to Córdoba, to its caves, to discover some lost echo in his childhood, but suddenly I realized it would be the same mistake as always. The only way to move and to know is to remain quiet, in silence. I would never find the poet in the eyes of Lupe, in his legend or in his family's home, though neither would I—I realized—in his works, the letters to his sister or his purported suffering. Cuesta was the image that I held onto with my gaze, the shadows, my mind, the devastated intelligence that linked us. Cuesta was, perhaps, my own pain.

I cried, cried as I'd never cried. My tears fell into the void. I ran to the bathroom and opened the faucet. Again I heard the water run till it vanished. With difficulty I took off my clothes as if each piece were to turn into a stone, lapidating me, and gazed listlessly at the penis hanging between my legs. It seemed so strange for the secrets of death to reside in that sad skin. What a pity: the blade with its brightness of rain didn't even cross my mind. I advanced forward on the floor tiles and allowed the stream to freely fall over my body. Like entering without god into the darkness of the sea.

2

I feel pain, rage, and shame. I want to put my thoughts in order, cool off. I can't understand why he changed so much, how he became transformed and consumed himself so suddenly: nothing remains of him, I hardly know him. Tell me, what makes a man go mad and fall apart? Or was he always that way and I just figured it out now? Tell me, please, why is it I hate him so much?

I can't stand myself. I must forget him; forget him even if I die. But I can't rid myself of his eyes fixed on my skin nor his semen running between my legs: they sully me like his face covered with make-up. I wouldn't be able to remove his filth though I'd wash a thousand times. By God, his figure follows me. I still have him by my side, sweaty and aroused. I'm so disgusted.

At the same time, the idea that I may be partly to blame tortures me. I left him, I couldn't tolerate him. He only had me, I was the only one capable of helping him, and instead, I'm here with you. Though I abhor him, though I could never go back to him, I still go on missing him, pitying him. At bottom perhaps I feel too responsible. On the other hand, I'm sure that even if that night hadn't happened nevertheless our life together didn't have a chance. I'd already made my decision and was planning to tell him when he came home. Perhaps he sensed it and that's why he behaved as he did.

I'm terrified.

Though you may not want to hear it I'm going to tell you about it.

3

Alma has left. There's no light, the phone remains disconnected, the door locked; the only sound that keeps me company is an incessant dripping from the bathroom sink. Its sound multiplies in concentric circles throughout the empty rooms. I hide in the study. I don't know where the others are or if they still exist: I don't care. I want to rest. My body is consumed; I don't wish anything else other than to rest. But it's impossible. I'm awake!

A glow from outside invades the silhouette of my hand. I spread my papers on the desk: they're useless notes, a copy of *The Magisterium of Jorge Cuesta* and a poem. I tear the loose sheets of my notebook, look at the essay and also rip it apart. I tear three sheets from my notebook and place them on top of the dresser. I haven't shaved, but it's already late. I'm standing before I become silent, and I write.

4

You know it perfectly: there are few things I hate more than writing, to rend myself in phrases that I hardly feel as mine. I relapse in spite of the various times I've sworn to you the opposite; I accept that I cannot avoid this test, that before I sink into the abyss of immortality I must adjust this last account with you. I have said it before: confession is the way I've found to save myself; hundreds of words that only await one of yours to bring comfort to my soul. I'm calm, in peace. Nothing bothers me any longer outside of the deaf shouts that I hurl on the paper. I have the confidence of one who assumes himself defeated and has decided not to search any longer, certain of the impossibility of a meeting. Or better, of its irreversibility, the suffocating fact which shows that we don't have any other option than the freedom of desire.

I'm aware that nothing of what I say will show you what is really in me, but at least I insist on this, that behind the obsolete sentences you may find a meaning, a wisp of truth. I'm not making any excuses for my inability to talk at length: I simply want you to be aware that I've made the greatest possible effort: since this mute and doomed story began, I've done nothing but try to talk with you. My body, my voice, my works, these paragraphs themselves that I dedicate, only have attempted to converse. That is the value of each instant in my life: I realize it, sadly too late. All I've said, written or thought has been because of you and for you, so that you liberate me from myself. Each syllable has replaced a tear, or a kiss. I wish you'd understand, but I know the humiliating failure to which language brings me, this pen, and this saliva. How to express the inexpressible…? How to say I love you so that it rings true? How to say I love you and that it may pain me? Months, years, centuries of crossing out scribbles, of enunciating sounds that deceive, separate, debase. What good are all those read books, the pronounced languages? In any way, my life is yours. If you don't want to have anything to do with me it's also yours; but if you don't want it, it's not mine nor anyone's any longer. It's late to understand that it's better to be silent. That everyone's worth is the same as everyone else's. That silence hurts like death. It is late for everything. For living. At last I knew, I understood the secrets, and learned that they're not useful. What's eternity and intelligence for, when you're alone? I've sought the exit door to time without ascertaining that in reality, behind formulas and sonnets, substances and mirrors, pleasure and anguish, I only desired you. Look at me closely and see that I haven't been violent against you, but for you. That I've been violent, you see, against what you were letting me hide, which diminished my love for you. I adore you, nothing in me ceases adoring you, and nothing in me can say I don't love you. Though I may keep it quiet, though I may not say it to you, though it might kill me, though you may not hear it, though no one may know it or see it, that it is the truth. And nevertheless I've shown the opposite: that nothing links a person to another one, that no bond is authentic. The past, what one does to retain someone else, is a mirage. No one deserves something based on what he has done for someone else. No one can justly make a claim; no one has the right to forgive that which is for someone else. Loneliness evades itself each moment. Nothing of ours exists: it vanished with my forgetfulness and my indifference, my madness. I'm to blame. It's not worth crying. Without realizing it, instead, I've reached what I never wanted, what at bottom I didn't wish. I'm the bearer of supreme knowledge, of the most terrible arcane for which human beings have struggled from the beginning. I, the saddest of alchemists, have in my power the undisputable truth, the final revelation. After so many unproductive outings, failed experiments, encounters, visits, lectures: after this interminable blind pain, I've pressed the answer between my lips. It isn't through the union of what is separate, or the comparison of beings, or the conjugation of the sexes in one body that one brushes against wisdom. The answer is different and we've known it since the beginning, but we are not aware of it more than once in our lifetime. Now it's my turn to embrace it, crunch it in the hand. That's why I abhor it and disdain it. Nothing erases it, nothing undoes it; neither the most violent ideas, nor the hardest impressions. Everything is combined in it and is formed with it. Paradoxically, in its center lies the meaning of the infinite: the only possible infinite. It doesn't last nor does it rest. The tense and musical air waits. There is a way to be outside of time, of overcoming it; a way to placate fleeing pleasure and the will that distances itself. That is the fruit of which time is master. It means to leave it all behind, to sacrifice it all, and to abandon it all.

To forever be without you. Forever alone. Throughout eternity.

Beloved, you are present in spite of the dark silence,

Jorge.

5

I recover my vigor and start again, counting in my mind, trying to expand seconds, without giving in to the perturbation. I continue the movement as if it were natural and imperceptible. I don't surrender to the temptation of thinking about her, I don't believe in her existence. I attempt to divert my attention with my only goal of distracting myself.

Cuesta. I want to stop his story though in the end I may not get to understand a passion such as his. It's useless; I'm nothing more than a forced copy, a sad imitator that doesn't get to brush by him. He acted, and regretted and suffered; I only pretend to act and regret and suffer: in vain, boredom impels me to this rotten adventure. I don't even dare…

I close my eyes, I choke back the spasm, and open them again; I'm nude in the darkness of my bedroom, but the cold comes from inside me and not from the floor. My numb arm hurts and I'm not capable of making my thoughts flow in another direction. I double the abuse; I seek to hurt myself, to empty myself of Alma, to expel her from my body.

A new failed attempt: my barely wet fingers, dribbling, and my flesh tenuously black and blue. I need to start again, from the beginning.

In spite of my tiredness I still desire her. That's what kills me, and makes me stay here, wasting away. I have to destroy her ghost, to get out of my skin the last drop of my love for her.

I lean against the wall; take hold of my sullied legs and place my forehead on my knees like a catafalque. I imagine I can observe myself from above, degraded voyeuristic god, and see my body wrecked and frail. It revolts me. I'll never possess Cuesta's dignity, his conviction, or his grief. I caress myself and remember Alma's lips as if they've felt pity for my genitals: the minimum to continue the martyrdom.

What I've done to her, the worse thing I've done, comes to mind; I don't even regret it. New deception: I think I deserve the lowest when I haven't overcome the hatred of a moment. Even in that violence there was a limit, a hidden moral: my own suffering. Poor writer intent on perversity, never worthy of ignominy.

This time I take longer to recover, the previous pain weighs on me, I almost cannot turn my wrist, atrophied by the tension. Pity is set aside for Cuesta, for me disdain. To self-emasculate is the vague delirium of a demigod, instead of being on the floor, naked, dirtied with my own self...

Now I know: this whole Cuesta affair has been a lie. How do I dare argue that anything links me to this crazy and thirsty poet? Not even possessing his story or going into his sick brain would it be possible to attain redemption. I'm an observer, a spy of shadows; since I began to write—I don't cease being ridiculous, grotesque.

I visited Lupe Marín and Natalia Cuesta, the cemetery and the insane asylum; I read everything that has been written on the poet, I read his works: a path that untangled the motives of madness and intelligence, the alchemical and biographical meanings previously unexplored. A diaphanous and absolute plan. A work of art ready to repeat itself: the structure of a perfect novel. To link myself with Cuesta, to relate Alma to Lupe and Natalia and even Horacio Barrientos with Diego Rivera;

to follow the path of his insanity. The cycle calling me to a story line that surpasses me, link of a chain that repeats itself and makes me immortal—finally immortal, like him—sacrificing my uniqueness for the sake of myth. A perfect novel and an equally useless life. I refuse to accept it. I prefer my own fragmented history, unserviceable, hypocritical, vain, the futility of my effort, my sad relationship with Alma, my one and unrepeatable Alma, and a destiny that cannot aggrandize me, that in no way resembles Cuesta's passion, that is as worthless as anyone else's, but that is enough to cry and finish.

I spill again on my feet and think about her. Perhaps that is the only thing that overcomes absurdity. Only for her image, for her remoteness, I acquiesce to write an ending.

6

She has left; there doesn't remain even a trace. Not even a memory, or a light. Her shadow has been transformed into the word that burns.

7

I lie down on the bed, pale and frail, my hands hidden under the sheets, sweetly placed on my belly. I resemble a statue beginning to emerge from the marble of the bed, in any case one more piece in the furniture assemblage of the room and not a living person. It's not even noticeable when my lungs expand or when my eyelids close at times. Nevertheless, an uncertain brightness escapes from my stare, as if in my broken and wrecked body, there still remained a residue of peace, of the secret fire that always nourished me.

Around me the whiteness is dense and infinite, a blinding pulchritude: floor, ceiling, walls, don't stand apart from the intolerable luminosity. Even the most minimum shadow has been annihilated, not a single corner has been made available to the reach of darkness. I've forbidden myself the only rest a man has a right to have: sleep.

I resist and try to forget, but the reflectors, carefully positioned, prevent me from doing so; not without the intent of punishment I've condemned myself to wakefulness. This is a good image of the eternity I've sought for so long: there isn't movement, tension, or flux, space itself dilutes into a mirror without edges. Only in a place like this, outside of the world, can a creature like me remain. The neutral ambiance is designed for my neutral body.

What do I think now that fate has transported me? What do I feel? Shame? Pain? Fear? Perhaps a crude sense of remorse, vainly directed, whose cause I ignore. In my face—I imitate the paleness of the angels—there's not a word to be read any longer, not a single accusation, not a single human feature. I've become another cause of silence: impossible to endow my actions with meaning. The best thing is to remain silent.

I rise with great effort, stand up and then kneel on the floor, next to the window. On my knees on the floor, I bring my hands together in front of my chest, under my chin, pursuing my childhood's fervor. But I don't get even a drop of the tears that moved me at the time. Instead of a prayer a prolonged trembling caresses my sealed lips, a slow breeze that doesn't transfigure into sound. Instead, internally I pray with authentic zeal though my prayers crash against the ceiling.

Lord, our destiny is written from the beginning, I write in a piece of paper addressed to Alma. I remember her eyes and I love her desperately. I want to hold onto her gaze, save myself with it. How could we avoid it? We are subjugated to it, and with no shelter other than your mercy. I want to shout but my mouth tastes of ash. My skin oozes each syllable, each letter: Oh Lord, our God, may you want to guard us with it, not leaving unprotected any of us who are your servants.

How long did I stay on my knees, carrying out a deaf and useless penitence? How many years in that agony? My slow breathing extinguishes time; the distance between inhalations and exhalations dilate the minutes. Thought is not subjugated to the passing of time.

Finally I decide. From the street shouts that make the walls vibrate can be heard. An incomprehensible voice seeks my freedom. Noises weigh on me; I wish that silence keeps me company once and for all. Not even distant pain moves me; sensations have vanished. I don't feel, nor remember, nor suffer, nor cry. Almost instinctually, by inertia, I tie some sheets to the headboard of the bed. The taste darkness distills is the proper sense, that inhabits others and dominates the future.

Mexico City, 1989/1992

AUTHOR'S NOTE

AFTERWORD

BIBLIOGRAPHY

ACKNOWLEDGEMENTS

Author's Note

In Spite of the Dark Silence contains numerous passages from Cuesta's works; the majority are part of the narrative, though some are actual citations. Fragments of his poems are from the collection compiled by Luis Mario Schneider and Miguel Capistrán (*Poemas y Ensayos*, vol. 1; see Bibliography), except for indications to the contrary. Passages from his correspondence are excerpted from the collection assembled by Héctor Pérez Rincón in *La Gaceta del Fondo de Cultura Económica*, no. 194 (February 1987), unless stated otherwise. Below is a list of the most important references[1]:

In spite of the dark silence
(*Letter* to Natalia Cuesta, cit. by Panabière, *Itinerario de una disidencia* [FCE, México, 1983], p. 54)

I awaken in me what I've been / to become silence and nothing.
(*Sonnet*, incipit "A wanderer I am without meaning")

That is the fruit of which time is master,
("Song to a Mineral God", v. 217)

---

1. Citations and Cuesta's verses translated by Olivia Maciel Edelman.

Lord, our destiny is written since the beginning of time…
without leaving unprotected those of us who are your servants
("Prayer")

The taste that darkness distills / is the proper sense, that inhabits others / and dominates the future
("Song…" vv. 220-223)

To joy into which the instant turns / the thirst that desires it survives
("Sonnet", idem)

It is life to be there, so fixedly, / as the icily transparent height / pretends to to be for anything that climbs
("Song…" vv. 36-38)

There isn't solidity that such pressure can resist
("Song…" v. 48)

I don't want to disdain you as I don't want to love you
(*Letter* from Lupe Marín to Jorge Cuesta)

The sight in space diffused, / is space itself…
("Song…" v. 30)

Let chance test me in this absurd journey; I will try my luck in it
(*Letter* to Lupe Marín)

Nothing can make me keep from you…Allow me to defend myself from dying
(*Letter* to Lupe Marín)

I have spoken to you, I speak to you candidly…All my life is crying for you,
(*Letter* to Lupe Marín)

Time doesn't stop, but passes; the image / dies, yes, that aspires
to what passes
("Sonnet", idem)

Death is vain, / profound and sad
("Sonnet", incipit "Oh, life—exist")

It's there, still hard, I don't yet leave it...Linked to what inter-
nal, profound agility
(*Letter*, cit by Nigel Grant Sylvester, *Vida y Obra de Jorge Cuesta*
[Premià, México, 1984], p. 24)

I see what is prolonged in time...what dilates
(*Letter*, cit. by Nigel Grant Sylvester, ibid.)

Let dense silence swallow the obscure black / rumor...
(*Canto*, vv. 198-199)

In eternal Samarkand...numid of organdi
("Poem" collected by Doctor Barona during the last internment
of Cuesta, cit. by Héctor Pérez Rincón, "The Death of a Poet",
in *Literatura y Psique*, UAM, México, 1990, p. 75)

...in a sleepy and quiet water / a face adventures
("Song..." vv 61-62)

...memory oppresses / of the opaque matter that.../ darkens...
("Song..." vv 92-94)

A wandering I am without sense
("Sonnet", idem)

My life is yours...and it isn't mine nor anybody's
(*Letter* to Lupe Marín)

I haven't been violent toward you...that is the truth
(*Letter* to Lupe Marín)

Nothing erases her...and it forms it with her
(*Letter*, cit. by Nigel Grant Sylvester, loc. cit.)

Nor lasts, nor reposes
("Canto..." v. 3)

The tense and musical air waits
("Song..." v. 216)

To the word that burns
("Song..." v. 203)

Afterword

Denso el silencio trague el negro obscuro
rumor, como el sabor futuro
sólo la entrada guarde
y forme en sus recónditas moradas,
su sombra ceda formas alumbradas
a la palabra que arde

Dense, may silence swallow the obscure black
rumor, as the future taste
may only guard the gate
and form in its most hidden dwellings,
its shadow ceding radiant forms
to the word that burns

> — Jorge Cuesta, "Canto a un dios mineral"
> ("Song to a Mineral God"), 1942

Jorge Volpi (who was born in Mexico City in 1968) is a member of the *Generation of the Crack Movement* (Crack meaning "rupture" as understood within the context of the Latin American Avant-Gardes). He co-authored with Eloy Urroz, Ignacio Padilla, Ricardo Chávez, and Pedro Ángel Palou, the *Manifiesto Crack* in the 1990s or in 1996. The "rupture" meant to part with cynical and superficial and outdated movements of the past.

Though the *Manifiesto Crack* recalls the powerful legacy of Cervantes, Kafka, Flaubert, Rulfo, Yañez, and Calvino, among others, it beckons a new literary spirit. The aesthetic that some texts by Cortázar or García Márquez (the renowned movement of *magic realism*) sparked no longer satisfied the thirst for renewal. Additionally, the *Crack* aesthetic reflects a sense of disappointment with civilization's progress. According to Ben Ehrenreich, *Crack* literature is permeated with a sense of disillusionment with the world of neo-liberal orthodoxy, whether of a post-national or post-ideological nature. Read: *In Search of Klingsor, The End of Madness*, or *Season of Ash*, also by Volpi. One could add to Ehrenreich's assertions that the disillusionment extends to an exaggerated belief in nationalisms, ethnocentric systems of thought based on religious thinking, and chauvinistic patriotisms.

In Volpi's first published novel, *In Spite of the Dark Silence* (*A pesar del oscuro silencio*, 1992), a new aesthetic form, a light displacement of syntax already exists in an embryonic stage, and it precedes the drafting of the *Crack Manifiesto*. This new syntax appears to be inspired by the neo-baroque style in which chemist-poet Jorge Cuesta, a member of the group *Los Contemporáneos* (1920s-1950s), wrote. Cuesta preoccupied himself with what he called the *poetries of vertigo*. Though this literary premise is worthy of greater analysis, for the purpose of this Afterword suffice it to say, that its innovation is absorbed and enriched, not solely by a group of poets but also by a group of novelists, the founders of the *Crack Movement*. While at this point it can rightfully be claimed that its main protagonists are Mexican writers, it is possible that this movement may yet gain adepts in other parts of Latin America. It is still too early to predict how this literary movement will evolve or whether it will remain essentially intrinsic to this specific group of Mexican novelists.

In Volpi's novel there are several instances in which the order of a more traditional syntax is altered, not only through the incorporation of fragments from Cuesta's poems, but also through the use of sentences or phrases, at times without either subject, verb, or predicate. Therefore, it's possible to find phrases such as the following ones: "Outside of time, outside of reason," "Immortality in an instant," "The hands, yes, of creators, light and turbid, Renaissance languid hands." Such phrasing at times, particularly in the Spanish, conveys a sense of euphoria in the letters written by the reconstructed Cuesta, whose life the protagonist (also named Jorge) is researching. At other times, the fragmentary syntax communicates the fears of the narrator, at the possibility of loosing his own self while progressively becoming more enmeshed with his subject of study, Cuesta the poet. That frustration of the protagonist rises to a crescendo in the monologue bemoaning the break-up with his lover Alma: "I'm standing, before I fall into total silence, and I write." Though the sentence maintains a subject (I), the second part of the sentence, due to its enigmatic nature, "before I fall into total silence," seems semantically displaced. It's not clear yet, in context, why it doesn't seem to make sense. It's only when the reader has encountered in the first chapter a reconstruction of the suicide of Jorge Cuesta, through the protagonist's vivid imagination, that the interior of the sentence, the "fall into total silence," rings true. The displacement of meanings through previously made sentences serves as a way of linking disparate spaces, times, and characters.

Phrases that originate in Cuesta's sonnets help convey a sense of epiphany within the character of "Cuesta" in the novel, and clarity of purpose to Jorge, the young writer protagonist: "I touched the humid clay, absorbed by the eloquent revelation: the sight in space diffused, is space itself".

These 'displacements of syntax,' which could be viewed as syntactical variations with subtle alterations of logic, at times, stay on this side of the poetic, and then suddenly cross into the seemingly nonsensical or irrational. The vibratory effect is so tenuous that it could be argued that Jorge Volpi didn't intend to create a new aesthetic in the novel, the 'aesthetic of displacement,' and that this came about only as a by-product of narrative process, perhaps by way of a "creative accident," or in some way through Cuesta's own voice as inspiration. But when these very real innovations to the more traditional syntax in Latin American literature are placed side by side with the *Crack Manifiesto,* it is evident that a new elixir has been created. The experimentation in *Dark Silence* with this new aesthetic had seemingly just begun, and was a precursor to the 'rupture' of *Crack* literature.

In the *Crack Manifiesto* Jorge Volpi writes: "Paraphrasing Nietzsche, the end of the world doesn't occur outside but inside our heart…We are beings multiple or divided, who doubts it? The point here is that only literature is capable of integrating us back with our ghosts, it makes it possible for the imaginary friends of adolescence to become real, or worse yet, authors of our days." It is as if literature were capable of accomplishing what the ancient alchemists had attempted to do, reconciling opposites, nullifying the antipodes, as Cuesta wanted.

Novelist Pedro Ángel Palou, another contributor to the *Crack Manifiesto,* states that *Crack* novels aren't born out of certainty but out of doubt, and are not written in the standardized language of television. "A Feast of language and why not, a new sense of the baroque; whether in the syntax, in the lexicon, or in the morphology." Interestingly enough, Palou also wrote a novelized biography of poet Xavier Villaurrutia (*In a World's Bedroom*, 2003). The baroque in that text is born out of the introduction of verses from Villaurrutia's poems into the prose. Jorge Volpi had independently achieved something similar a decade earlier with Jorge Cuesta's verses in *In Spite of the Dark Silence* (1992). Both, Xavier Villaurrutia and Jorge Cuesta, were members of the group *Contemporáneos*. Furthermore, whereas Villaurrutia wrote with a sense of penumbral surrealism, Cuesta's poems show a baroque construction, a type of tergiversation. *In Spite of the Dark Silence* boldly expresses a new prose; it is the result of language struggling to free itself from the straitjacket of a decrepit and worn out magical realism. The *Crack* movement had just begun to experience delight in the pleasure of Cuesta's golden flowers.

In his book *The Age of Wonder*, Richard Holmes writes about the 'wonder' that lit a fire in the mind of poets like Coleridge and drove him to attend Humphry Davy's lectures on the mysteries of electricity and other chemical processes. This was going to be a way for Coleridge to "enlarge his stock of metaphors." Like Cuesta, Coleridge believed that science was imbued with the 'passion of hope.' Unlike Coleridge, Cuesta pursued the realm of the esoteric as well as of the chemical to reach eternal life. Cuesta belongs to that long line of scientist-artists which in the Renaissance included the likes of Leonardo Da Vinci, Luca Pacioli, and Nicholas of Cusa. The reconciliation of the opposites, an important alchemical concept for surrealists such as André Breton, took hold in Cuesta´s mind, and led him to combine the material and the abstract; substances and words; a dangerous path which inclined him to experiments with his own body, by self-injecting enzymes. Volpi, in writing *In Spite of the Dark Silence*, attempted what Bakhtin called *vzhivanie,* where the author tries to enter into the life of his character without losing his own individuality. In contrast to empathizing, *vzhivanie* (better translated as *living into*), results in a type of spiritual enrichment. *In Spite of the Dark Silence* conveys a brief and agile narrative, which poses profound questions about aesthetics and science, philosophy and psychology, chemistry and alchemy. This semi-biographical novel manifests a precocious talent in the handling of language, and represents a serious attempt to innovate not just the lexicon, or the syntax of Mexican novels, but also their thematic content. Indeed, this is the first Mexican novel that approaches writing itself as a transformative process; in a metafictional sort of heightened awareness, Jorge, the protagonist, comes to the realization that writing is altering him. Additionally, this is the first Mexican novel that combines the themes of poetry (aesthetics) and science, and makes them the focus of inquiry. These are some of the reasons why despite its imperfections, if there are any, *In Spite of the Dark Silence* deserves a well earned place in the canon of Mexican and Latin American literature.

Jorge Volpi´s *In Spite of the Dark Silence* opens our eyes to the ever-changing fabric of a writer's world, to its schizophrenia, its dangers, to its 'hypochondriac crunch.' The reader experiences a type of *vzhivanie*, through *living into* Jorge's world. Jorge Volpi, along with other members of the *Crack* literary movement, begins a new conversation with the luminous and ever rare transubstantial word.

Olivia Maciel, 2010

Bibliography

Bretón, André. *Manifestoes of Surrealism*. Translated from the French by Richard Seaver and Helen R. Lane. Ann Arbor: University of Michigan Press, 1972.

Cuesta, Jorge. *Poemas y Ensayos*. Edited by Luis Mario Schneider and Miguel Capistrán. Mexico City: Universidad Nacional Autónoma de México, 1964.

Holmes, Richard. *The Age of Wonder*. New York: Pantheon Books, 2009.

Letras de México 3, no. 21 (September 15, 1942): 3–4.

Morson, Gary Saul. *Rethinking Bakhtin*. Evanston, IL: Northwestern University Press, 1989.

Poggioli, Renato. *The Theory of the Avant-Garde*. Translated from the Italian by Gerald Fitzgerald. Cambridge, MA: Belknap Press of Harvard University Press, 1968.

Palou, Pedro Ángel. *En la alcoba de un mundo*. Mexico City: Plaza y Janés, 2003.

Schneider, Luis Mario. *México y el surrealismo (1925–1950)*. Mexico City: Arte y Libros, 1978.

Volpi, Jorge. *A pesar del oscuro silencio*. Mexico City: Editorial Joaquín Mortiz, 1992.

Volpi, Jorge, Eloy Urroz, Ignacio Padilla, Ricardo Chávez, and Pedro Ángel Palou. "Manifiesto Crack." *Lateral Revista de Cultura,* no. 70 (October 2000).
http://www.lateral-ed.es/lema/070manifiestocrack.htm

Acknowledgments

I wish to acknowledge and thank Dr. Patrick O'Connor, professor and chair of Hispanic Studies at Oberlin College, for his insightful contributions to this translation; and grateful to Beatriz Margain, cultural attaché for the Consulate of Mexico in Chicago, and Professor Héctor García, Loyola University-Chicago, for their encouragement.

Swan Isle Press is an independent, not-for-profit, literary publisher
dedicated to publishing works of poetry, fiction and nonfiction
that inspire and educate while advancing the knowledge and
appreciation of literature, art, and culture. The Press's bilingual
editions and single-language English translations
make contemporary and classic texts more accessible to
a variety of readers.
For information on books of related interest or for
a catalog of new publications contact:

www.swanislepress.com

In Spite of the Dark Silence

Designed by Esmeralda Morales-Guerrero
Typeset in Calisto
Printed on 55# Glatfelter Natural